EL GRA RM

STAGECOACH TO WACO WELLS

Trouble is coming, and it's due to arrive on the night train into Dodge City. Marshal Ben Carter has seen gunmen gathering at the railhead, waiting for their boss to return on the mighty locomotive speeding through the wilderness towards them. The marshal knows he is no match for the deadly men gathered like vultures. It seems like time to run or die — until bounty hunter Johnny Diamond arrives, and Carter proposes they join forces . . .

MICHAEL D. GEORGE

STAGECOACH
TO WACO WELLS

Complete and Unabridged

LINFORD
Leicester

First published in Great Britain in 2014 by
Robert Hale Limited
London

First Linford Edition
published 2016
by arrangement with
Robert Hale Limited
London

A catalogue record for this book is available
from the British Library.

ISBN 978–1–4448–2933–4

Published by
F. A. Thorpe (Publishing)
Anstey, Leicestershire

Set by Words & Graphics Ltd.
Anstey, Leicestershire
Printed and bound in Great Britain by
T. J. International Ltd., Padstow, Cornwall

This book is printed on acid-free paper

*Dedicated with love and gratitude
to the memory of my father,
Denis John George*

Prologue

Pride is one of those strange emotions. It has always been so and shall continue that way until the end of time. Sometimes men choose to hide behind it as though it might save the innocent whilst others choose to use it in a vain attempt to protect themselves.

Whichever excuse they choose the truth is that pride has always been a destructive emotion. It gives men excuses to hide behind.

Yet those who hide behind its fragile shield usually discover that what they once considered a saving grace, they soon find to be a curse which could destroy them.

Pride has always gone before a fall and some men topple far further than even they imagined possible.

Marshal Ben Carter was such a man. He was cursed by pride. In his attempts to keep the citizens of Dodge City at bay and unaware of his secret he had isolated himself not only from their help but also from their friendship.

Carter soon discovered that he had isolated himself from every living person in Dodge City.

They had grown to despise him.

His refusal to allow any of them close to him in order to protect his secret had backfired. Carter had become the victim of his own curse.

When it became common knowledge that the notorious outlaw Jonas Stokes was returning to Dodge to avenge his imprisonment by killing Carter the intrepid lawman had to try to overcome his pride and ask for the help of the very same people who hated him.

Pride had proved to be a fallacious shield.

Would it add another victim to its tally?

1

Dodge City was crackling with the coming of another sunset. It seemed as if everyone in town knew that soon blood would flow down its walls on to the dry streets. There was a common awareness that danger was heading towards the town. A rumour had spread like wildfire through Dodge and all of its expectant citizens knew where it had originated. The telegraph worker had a loose tongue when well lubricated with red-eye and there were always plenty of folks willing to provide the potent spirit in exchange for personal information.

The telegraph operator had delivered his wire less than ten minutes after it arrived. Then he had roamed the town's numerous drinking holes and repeated the message word for word for free liquor.

The man who had received the

daunting message addressed to him was not so lucky. He had read its words and slowly died as the gravity of his situation gradually dawned upon him.

He had been warned of his own impending demise. For what seemed an eternity the telegraph wire had remained on his desk blotter as his eyes studied its ominous words over and over again. No matter how many times Carter read those words of warning he seemed unable to do anything.

His mind had melted inside his skull.

Town Marshal Ben Carter was afraid as from his office window he watched the sun slowly setting. Finally his bluff was being called and he knew he would be found lacking against a real gunfighter. He had rocked on his chair and stared blankly at his gloved right hand for more than an hour and still the dread continued to haunt him.

Carter was like a man possessed by demons.

Not demons like those that crawled

from their graves up on Boot Hill when darkness fell, but the kind that never quit festering inside the craw of someone who had begun to realize that his time was just about up.

His mouth and throat felt as though he had swallowed barbed wire. They grew dryer with each tick of his wall clock. No amount of coffee could moisten his palate. The Grim Reaper already had a noose around his neck and he knew it.

Carter mulled over the telegram like a man who had already been shot to ribbons but had not yet decided to fall. He thought of how he had sent the villainous outlaw to prison when most men of his profession might have simply killed the critter. Why had he not killed him when he had had a chance? It had been a mistake that now came back to haunt him. His gloveless left hand toyed with the small scrap of paper.

It was his death certificate.

At last Carter rose from his chair.

Terror gripped his soul and there was nothing he could do apart from run. Yet Carter was not a man to run away from the monsters that filled him with fear.

He was cut from a different cloth.

Since the day he'd strapped his first gunbelt around his hips he had never high-tailed it away from a problem, no matter how tortuous it had appeared. Ben Carter had always faced his enemies head on.

Sweat trailed freely down his face.

Yet for all his courage Carter had good call to flee. Of all the souls in Dodge he alone had good reason not to remain in town.

The stalwart marshal had never chosen the easy option, though. Pride was a sturdy trait but also one that was foolhardy.

Again his eyes looked at his gloved gun hand.

The tall, rangy figure stood inside his office staring through the window at the hundreds of people who continued to pass.

Carter noticed that for some reason each and every one of them briefly glanced in his direction as they made their way in various directions. A cold chill traced his sweat-soaked spine. Somehow they were all aware of the news he had received and were anticipating his fate with cold derision.

There were no encouraging smiles. Nothing but scornful eyes stared at him. The only other emotion any of the countless faces showed the marshal was icy contempt. Carter was well aware that none of the hundreds of people in Dodge would shed a tear over his passing. In fact they would relish the sight of his being cut down after he'd been torn to bits by a gunfighter's weaponry.

All any of them wanted was a good spectacle. A magnificent show, which they could tell their offspring about in the coming years.

Folks were like that, his tormented mind kept telling him. They all enjoyed seeing a good fight. The bloodier it was the better they liked it.

Carter had never seen a hanging that had not drawn a huge crowd. The women and children seemed to like that sort of thing the most.

Sweat trailed down his face.

He knew that death came easily in the West. He had witnessed it many times and now it seemed as though it was his turn to walk hand in hand with the Grim Reaper. Again his confused mind vainly tried to think of a solution to his problem.

There must be something he could do to save his skin.

There had to be.

Carter ran his large fingers through his mane of grey hair as his eyes continued to stare out into the street. Fate had him gripped tightly in its grasp and there was nothing he could do but accept it.

For three years he had been the marshal at Dodge. Three years during which he had managed to save more than $200 but as his eyes narrowed he began to realize that he should have spent every last dime of it on cheap booze and even cheaper females.

Now it seemed too late.

His mind flashed back to the eventful day when the outlaw had roamed into town with guns blazing. Carter recalled how he had been lucky that day and managed to drop a hundred-pound bag of animal feed from the loft window of the livery stable down on to the head of the crazed gunman.

Jonas Stokes had fallen in a heap under the weight. He had been knocked senseless by the unexpected impact. Carter had used the valuable time that followed to descend and hog-tie Stokes.

The marshal swallowed hard. 'I should have killed him,' he whispered.

The office grew darker.

For a brief moment Carter considered striking a match and touching the wick of his desk lamp but something told him that that might be a mistake.

His eyes returned to the wall clock.

Its black hands on the white face told

him all he needed to know. It was nearly seven in the evening and death was coming to town on the eight o'clock passenger train from Yuma. Death with all its finality would soon make its visitation and he would greet it helplessly.

Carter knew that he had roughly an hour before the train arrived. Barely enough time to write a will. His eyes glanced down at the blotter and the small telegraph message lying on its ink-stained surface. The room was now too dark to read the ominous words but terror had engraved them into his memory for ever.

It read that the train was due to arrive at eight and that it had a very special passenger aboard, named Jonas Stokes. One who had vowed to return to Dodge one day and kill him. That day had arrived.

Carter sighed heavily. He considered walking out of his office and heading to the livery stable. He wondered how many sturdy mounts they had there and, if he rode away from Dodge, what were his chances of escaping his would-be executioner's wrath.

The trouble with Carter was that he had never been much of a horseman. His job in town meant that he rarely had call to ride anywhere. He doubted if he could outride anyone as determined as the man he knew was heading towards the town to kill him.

The lawman stared out into the street. Stokes had been duly released from prison. He had served his time. Carter watched as a man lit the street lanterns. One by one the amber illumination of the coal tar erupted inside the glass boxes and cast its strange hue upon everything within its limited range. It was like watching giant fireflies coming to life.

His mind raced again as it attempted to find a way out of his predicament. There had to be a way.

He considered the numerous times that he had scraped a dead body off the town's streets in the three years he had been in office. So many times that he had lost count. On how many occasions had he plucked a bullet-riddled gambler off the floor of a saloon or gaming-house and hauled the limp carcass to the undertaker's office?

That meant nothing to the faces that glanced at him as they passed the office. That was what he was paid to do.

Once more he looked at his gloved right hand and sighed.

Not once had he had to face anyone with his Colt .45 in those three uneventful years. The people in Dodge City had never seen him draw and there was a very good reason for that.

He never had because he was unable.

Like a poker player with only two fives, he had bluffed everyone into thinking he could use his useless hand.

Ben Carter had managed to conceal that simple fact from each and every one of the folks who had voted him into office. Three years of deceit had finally come to haunt the lone lawman.

It was not that he was a coward. He

had proved his gun skills years before and had once been considered one of the fastest draws in the territory.

That had been before his gun had been shot from his hand, leaving it permanently crippled.

Sadly, Carter glanced down at his gloved right hand. The brutal truth of why he wore the leather glove was unknown to everyone in Dodge City. Only the lawman knew the details and he had never revealed those to anyone.

He peeled back the leather glove and stared through the gloom of the darkening room at the hideous claw which was all that remained of his once flexible hand. The scars of the missing fingers stared back at him. That was the truth about Ben Carter.

Two random bullets had destroyed the hand for ever.

He shook his head.

Carter thought about the people of Dodge. They would never have hired him if they had known that his gun hand was totally useless. Who hires a cripple to become town marshal? He tried to move his remaining fingers but there was no response to his mental commands.

The two brutal shots that had severed the bones had also managed to cut the tendons to his remaining fingers. His hand had become virtually useless but he had somehow managed to fool everyone in town that there was nothing wrong.

Carter could use his thumb, but that was about it. How does a gunman fire a six-shooter when half of his glove's fingers are empty of everything except padding?

That had been five years ago but the memory was still vivid. It was branded into his very soul. He had tried to learn how to use his gun with his left hand but, like most right-handed folks, he was clumsy with it.

So he had kept up the masquerade and let those who watched him going about his daily rituals believe that there was nothing wrong.

His eyes returned to the clock.

It continued to tick.

It was a relentless reminder that death was coming with each passing moment. Each tick of that clock meant he had a second less to live.

He recalled how a shackled Jonas Stokes had screamed revenge from the barred wagon they were taking him away in. Now the outlaw was returning to make those words come true.

A cold shiver traced his every fibre. Ben Carter paced around the office like a caged animal. Every instinct screamed to him that the only sensible thing to do was to get his horse and ride as far away from Dodge as possible.

Ben Carter knew only too well that a man can never run away from himself. He pulled the black leather tightly back over his scarred hand and plucked his Stetson off the stand. He placed his hat on his grey hair and inhaled deeply.

The lawman opened the office door and stepped out on to the boardwalk. His eyes looked along the street of red-brick and wooden buildings to where the train depot stood.

The setting sun made its tracks gleam.

'Howdy, Marshal,' someone innocently said as he passed the lawman.

With a forced smile Carter touched the brim of his hat and made a slight bow.

He started to make his rounds.

Carter had taken just three steps when the church clock struck the hour. The entire street resounded to the chimes as they rang out over and over again. Carter glanced down to the further end of Front Street and stared at the church's whitewashed tower. His eyes focused on the clock face.

It was now seven o'clock.

With any luck the lawman had an hour left to live. Carter continued to walk down the busy thoroughfare as every particle of his being told him to ride. There were towns in every direction from Dodge City. Places where men who did not want to be found could hide, but that was not the lawman's way.

In all his days he had never run away from anyone or anything, and he was not about to start now. Running away from one monster usually meant that you ended up running straight into an even worse one.

Marshal Ben Carter continued to walk slowly down the street with his useless, black-gloved hand hovering above a holstered Colt .45 that he knew he could never draw.

Pride was a hard thing for a man to shake himself free of.

2

The streets were busy, yet as Ben Carter walked down them the crowds parted before him. He suddenly knew how Moses must have felt when faced with the Red Sea. The lone marshal placed a cigar between his dry lips and scratched a match down a porch upright. As he paused to suck in its flame his gaze darted across the faces of the men and women who were still wandering along the long thoroughfare. None of them seemed disturbed to know that they were looking at a man who was already doomed.

He exhaled a line of smoke and flicked the match out into the street. There was not a scrap of sympathy in any of the faces he studied.

The townsfolk were excited, though.

They were excited at the prospect of seeing a gunfight and the slaying of a man in all its gory detail. Carter knew that in all the years he had worn a tin star and defended the people of Dodge City he had never got close to any of these faces. He knew most of their names but that was as close as Carter had come to any of them. Carter had never allowed anyone to get close to him, no matter who it was. When a man has a secret such as his, he reasoned, it is best if he remains alone.

When he had entered the election to take on the job of town marshal Carter had already been severely crippled but his reputation as tough gun-fighter had gone before him. What the citizens of Dodge had seen was what they had wanted and expected to see.

Carter had decided three years earlier that unless he cared for his secret to become common knowledge it was far wiser to remain distant from every person in Dodge. The closer someone is to an individual the more chances that individual has of discovering all of one's secrets.

He had never dropped his guard for one second in all of that time, for fear of anyone learning the truth. To him it had been vital to maintain that illusion and yet, as he drew even more cigar smoke deep into his lungs, he began to wonder how wise he had been.

Carter knew that his demise would not be mourned.

It was a sad and telling truth. Now it was too late. He had no friends in the entire town. There was nobody upon whom he might call to help him in his determination to survive.

Not one solitary person.

With his cigar gripped between his teeth Ben Carter crossed the busy street between the passing horsemen. With each step he recalled the last deputy he had managed to hire. That had been more than six months earlier. The town council had agreed that he could hire two deputies but that had never come to be.

The last deputy had abruptly quit, like all of the others.

Carter stepped up on to the board-walk outside the bakery. He knew it was now far too late to hire anyone new and far too late to make any friends.

He was truly alone.

He stood in the shadows of the porch overhang and watched the passing people. He had never seen so many people before at this time of the evening. Usually after sundown the town grew quieter but not tonight. He wondered whether they were only still out on the street to watch him being gunned down.

It was an unnerving thought.

The aroma of baking bread wafted from within the locked store. He knew that the flour-dusted man inside the bakery would work all through the hours of darkness so that Dodge would be well supplied with his wares when dawn arrived.

The troubled lawman brooded about the things he could not alter. He stared at the glowing red tip of the cigar in his left hand and watched its smoke rise up to the wooden roof shingles above his head.

He wondered if he would see the sun rise again, or would his body be cold long before sunrise.

A gambling man would not have given him odds but Carter had survived a long time by defeating the odds. He tapped the ash from the smoke and raised his head until his neck clicked, reminding him that he was still alive. He pondered his future.

Every clock in Dodge gave him an hour to live.

What did clocks know? he asked himself. They just ticked men's lives away and continued to keep ticking until their springs broke or somebody forgot to wind them.

Carter removed his hat and mopped his brow on his shirtsleeve. He then ran the fingers of his left hand through his hair and returned the hat to his greying locks.

Suddenly two shots echoed all around the lawman.

Abruptly Carter swung on his heels and glanced around at the hundreds of faces that looked expectantly back at him. Every face had imagined witnessing the marshal crumple and fall into a bloody heap when they also had heard the startling gunshots.

There was a look of profound disappointment in each of the faces as they watched the surprised lawman.

Carter stepped down into the street and looked all around him. Then another shot shook the very fabric of the town's buildings. He instantly knew where the shot had come from.

'That came from the Long Branch,' he said, and he started to run towards the distant saloon.

Again the crowd parted as the intrepid lawman ran through them. Carter did not slow his pace until he reached the edge of the boardwalk outside the saloon. The aroma of gunsmoke floated out from its doorway. It drifted with the stink of stale liquor and cigar smoke over and under the swing doors of the notorious drinking hole.

Raised voices replaced the sound of gunfire inside the Long Branch.

The tall lawman came to a sliding halt close to the saloon's swing doors as dozens of men and women raced out into the relative safety of the main thoroughfare.

Carter edged closer to the swing doors as they rocked on their hinges. He narrowed his eyes as he peered over the doors into the still-busy saloon.

He had pinpointed the cause of the trouble.

A score of hefty men encircled a thin man dressed in a tailored, long black coat and a neat, flat-brimmed hat. The lawman instantly recognized the man as one of two gamblers who had arrived by stagecoach only two days earlier.

The angry mob were raging at the gambler.

The gambler in turn was holding a smoking five-inch-barrelled .45 in his hand as he slowly but surely backed away from them.

Ben Carter could not see any bodies but knew from experience that it was only a matter of time before there were some.

The marshal rested his gloved hand on the top of the swing doors and pushed them inwards. He entered and with no hint of concern for his own safety he continued to walk towards the men.

A cloud of gunsmoke drifted above the crowd.

Noticing that the marshal had arrived in the saloon the burly men moved aside and allowed him to stand between the arguing factions. Carter rested his useless gloved hand on the holstered gun as he reached the trapped gambler.

He turned to face the mob.

'What's going on here?' Carter yelled out above the sound of the bellowing crowd. 'Somebody better speak up or I'll pistol-whip you all.'

A man who seemed to be as wide as

he was tall edged towards the stern-faced lawman. He had blood trailing from the corner of his mouth and more than a few teeth missing. He aimed a stumpy finger at the gambler.

'That dude is a card sharp, Marshal,' the bleeding man announced. 'Arrest the dude. Look what he done to my face. He hit me with his gun.'

'Stop snivelling. You've had a lot worse,' Carter told the wide-girthed figure. 'Hell, I've seen your wife beat you up a whole lot worse than that.'

The gambler aimed the gun at the crowd. 'They was gonna hang me, Marshal.'

Before the lawman could say anything in response the .45 blasted a shot from its still-smoking barrel. Carter swung back and slapped the gambler with his hat.

'Stop shooting your gun, dude. You'll hit something if you keep squeezing on that damn trigger. Put that gun away or I'll make you sit on it,' Carter growled.

The gambler looked down his painfully sharp nose at the lawman and argued.

'If I holster my gun this bunch of cannibals will tear me to shreds,' he said.

Carter raised an eyebrow, then slapped the thin man again with his hat. 'If you don't I'll get real ornery, stranger. Do you get my meaning? Am I being clear?'

'I'll kill the card sharp.' The larger, bleeding man took a swing at the gambler. The gambler screamed out and blasted his gun into the ceiling. Plaster showered all over everybody.

Carter felt debris landing upon his shoulders. He pushed the burly figure back and then turned to face the gambler. He snatched the smoking weapon from the gambler's hand and stuffed it in his own belt.

'Don't you move a muscle, dude,' Carter ordered. Then he returned his attention to the larger men. He scowled at them. 'Calm down and tell me what happened here.'

The bleeding man pointed at the gambler behind Carter.

'We caught him cheating, Marshal.'

'How did you catch him cheating?' Carter asked.

'We was playing poker and that thin bastard won,' the gruff man protested. 'He had to be cheating.'

'And there was the aces,' another of the grunting men added. 'How many damn aces are there in a deck of cards? He sure had more than four.'

Carter turned to face the thin gambler. He stepped close and glared into his eyes. They were ideal eyes for playing poker. They gave away nothing.

'And what's your story?' Carter pressed. 'Were you cheating or not?'

'I'm totally innocent, Marshal,' the gambler asserted. 'This is just a misunderstanding. I was lucky and this man attacked me. I had to defend myself, didn't I?'

Ben Carter had umpired many similar disputes. He knew exactly what had to be done to prevent any further shooting and bloodshed.

'The way I see it the pot belongs to our fat friend here.' Carter pointed at the bleeding man.

The burly man grunted with satisfaction.

'That's not fair,' the gambler grumbled. 'I won that pot fair and square.'

The lawman shook his head. His eyes narrowed.

'Hush up, dude. I'm fining you the value of your winnings.' The lawman grabbed the gambler's string tie and led him out of the Long Branch like a dog on a leash.

The gleeful mob fell on to the sawdust covered floor and began scooping up the poker chips.

The thin gambler continued to protest until they reached the street, where Carter released his grip on the tie. The lawman then shook the bullets from the weapon he had confiscated and returned it to the gambler.

'I'd take the next stagecoach out of here if I was you,' Carter advised firmly. 'Dodge ain't healthy for card sharps like you.'

'I'm no card sharp,' the gambler mumbled as he slid the empty weapon back into its concealed holster.

Ben Carter grabbed the thin man's arm. He smiled, then shook it violently. Two aces fell from the sleeve of the expensive jacket. Each man looked at the other.

'You're innocent, are you?' Carter asked wryly.

'I'll do as you advise, Marshal,' the gambler said sheepishly. He touched the brim of his hat and disappeared into the crowd.

Carter struck another match to relight his cigar. He watched as the smoke trailed the fleeing gambler, then turned and started his walk again.

The cool evening air somehow aided his attempt to think about his overriding problem. At last his brain was alive and he was determined to find a way out of his predicament. For an hour fear had gripped him, but now Carter seemed to be regaining both his courage and his faith in himself.

Carter looked down the street. His eyes focused on a wooden shingle hanging from a porch. The light from the store beamed out across the well-trodden street.

The shingle read, 'Leather Goods'.

The store sign lured the lawman like a moth to a naked flame.

The marshal strode towards it as a vague idea took form inside his head. He reached the leather-goods store and marched straight in. The storekeeper glanced up over his counter at the lawman. His expression altered when he set eyes upon Carter.

'Marshal Carter,' he stammered in stunned awe at the sight. It was the very first time he had seen the marshal enter his humble store.

Ben Carter gave a nod and approached the glass-topped counter and the nervous proprietor who stood behind it. His eyes studied the weapons inside the case as he rested his hands upon its glass surface.

'Looking for anything special, Marshal?'

The lawman did not answer straight away. He just studied Charlie Smith's wares. He moved away from the counter, then looked at the wall. It was full of the leather goods Smith was famed for. Everything from saddlebags to belts and holsters hung on the walls.

Unable to find what he sought Carter glanced at Smith.

'You got any left-handed gunbelts, Smith?' he asked.

Charlie Smith puzzled over the strange question posed by the marshal. A dozen thoughts flashed through his brain as he edged around the counter towards the tall figure. Yet no matter how much he thought about it, he came to no conclusions.

'We got one,' Smith said. He pointed to a belt hanging on a high nail. 'There ain't too much call for them in these parts, Marshal. I don't think I've met more than a dozen southpaws in twenty years.'

The lawman nodded. 'Get the belt down. I wanna check it.'

Smith obliged the lawman and reached up. He unhooked the well-crafted leather gunbelt and holster and handed it to the marshal.

'Is there any reason that you wanna look at it, Marshal?' Smith enquired.

'There is.' Carter studied the belt in his hands, then flashed a look at Smith. 'I'm going to buy it.'

Smith smiled. 'What in tarnation for? A left-handed gunbelt ain't much use for a right-handed *hombre*.'

Once more the lawman did not reply immediately. He unbuckled his own belt and handed it to the storekeeper. He swung the left-handed belt around his hips and then buckled it.

'But you ain't a southpaw, Marshal,' Smith remarked.

'I know, Smith.' Carter moved the holster around until it was perched on his right hip. A smile marked his usually expressionless face. The holster was facing backwards. Ideal for a cross draw.

Smith pulled the six-shooter from the holster of Carter's belt and handed it to the marshal. He watched as the lawman slid it in and out of the new holster. It was tight and got stuck against the unyielding leather.

'I reckon the holster needs oiling, Marshal,' Smith said knowingly. 'It ain't ever been used before and it's a tad dry.'

Carter looked at Smith. 'Get the oil. I want this holster so oiled up the gun will almost slide out into my hand.'

The expert leather worker oiled the holster, then removed the bullets from Carter's original belt and placed them into the new one.

Five minutes later the lawman seemed satisfied.

'This'll do just fine. I'll take it,' Carter whispered. He produced a wad of banknotes and peeled off a few. He handed them to Smith. 'You can keep my old belt.'

'But there ain't nothing wrong with it, Marshal,' Smith said as he opened his cash drawer. 'Are you sure?'

'Yep, I'm dead sure.'

Smith took a few coins from his cash drawer and turned to hand them back to the lawman, but Carter was gone. The lawman had returned to the street.

Charlie Smith rubbed his oily hands down his apron and walked to his front door. He still had no idea of why Carter had wanted the left-handed gunbelt. It did not seem to make any sense to the old leather worker. He watched the town marshal stroll down the boardwalk.

He closed the door and slid its bolt across to secure it. As his hands drew down the blinds he thought about the story that had been circulating in town for the previous hour.

Somebody was coming to Dodge City in order to kill Marshal Carter. That was what everyone was saying, and he had no reason to doubt a single word of it.

He shook his head of white hair, leaned over his lamp and blew out its flame.

'Good luck, Marshal.' He sighed quietly.

3

Smoke billowed from the chimney stack and floated over the large, dark engine. It enveloped the throbbing monster as the engine's powerful light sent a beam of shimmering illumination through the darkness. The huge locomotive was stationary as its guard drew down the chute from the water tower and started to replenish its boiler. The guard looked along the black body of the engine at the three passenger cars. Shafts of glowing lamplight beamed out of every window of the monster as it rested in the canyon. The line of gleaming tracks stretched out for endless miles in either direction.

The muscular guard kept a firm hold on the long rope which controlled the chute as gallons of water gushed down to replenish its tank. Even the fastest of trains were of little use if they could not make steam. As the water tank filled the magnificent engine hissed like a giant snake. It was ready to move again.

Strange reflections flickered across the side of a virtually flat rock face alongside the entire length of the train as the guard moved around the top of the engine.

Those inside the passenger cars of the train watched the odd movements of the guard as he went about his work on his perilous perch.

A dozen passengers struck up conversations as they realized that their long journey was almost at an end. Only one of their number remained aloof and totally silent. He had other things on his mind.

Ex-prisoner Jonas Stokes stared ahead with unblinking eyes. He saw none of his fellow passengers and did not hear one word of their various conversations.

Stokes was deep in thought.

No one who had set eyes upon the well-dressed middle-aged passenger since he had boarded the train back in Yuma gave him a second thought. Stokes was anything but the usual type of ex-convict. He looked unthreatening as he sat with his hands upon his knees, but looks were often deceptive.

Although Stokes had been sentenced to three years in prison for causing mayhem in Dodge City none of those who had set eyes upon his unassuming person had ever guessed the brutal truth of his past. In Dodge City no one had known that Stokes had actually slain at least a dozen men before he had ever reached Dodge.

Had they known of this the quiet man would never have walked free of the prison gates. In fact he would have more than likely had his neck stretched at the end of a rope.

Three years had seemed like a lifetime to Stokes.

Being caged like an animal had not done a thing to mellow his fiery nature. In fact it had fuelled his desire to kill again. Not just anyone but the one man who had accidentally managed to get the drop on him.

He had learned in prison the name of the man who had knocked him out and shackled him. As Jonas Stokes stared with cold eyes at his fellow passengers they did not know that Stokes was saying one name over and over again inside his warped mind.

Stokes was reciting the name of Ben Carter.

He had planned the execution of the lawman in his mind on every day of those three long years. The mentally sick outlaw had become totally deranged during his years of captivity.

There was no healing. There had been no transformation of an outlaw into a good person. Prison had rubbed salt in the wounds of Jonas Stokes.

Hatred had become an obsession.

In his mind Stokes had considered every means of achieving his goal. There were so many different ways in which a man could kill.

So many ways, but he was rationed to just one.

One solitary kill was not enough. Not for Stokes. He had thought of nothing else in his time in prison. He had to make the killing last as long as possible, his mind told him. There would be no swift end to Carter's life. It would have to be a slow, lingering process that brought Marshal Carter's existence to an end.

It seemed, in Stokes's twisted mind, to be a fitting demise for the lawman.

The train jolted suddenly.

Stokes inhaled as he heard a noise outside the window of the car. He snapped out of his increasingly horrific thoughts momentarily. Stokes glanced through the window of the car and saw the mooncast shadow of the water chute returning to the tower.

The entire locomotive shook. It grunted and groaned as if it were a living creature. Then Stokes heard the wheels spin and slowly the train started to move once more. The door at the end of the car opened and a man dressed in railroad blues entered.

The attendant walked between the seats. He smiled and spoke gently to the other seated passengers as he made his way towards the watching Stokes.

As the man neared where he was sitting Stokes raised a finger and attracted the attendant's attention. The smiling man with the dark-blue peaked hat paused.

'Can I help you, sir?'

'You surely can. When will we arrive in Dodge, partner?' Stokes asked the attendant. 'I've got me some mighty important business there.'

The man leaned against the rocking benches in the gently moving car. He pulled a silver watch from his pocket and flicked open its lid. He studied the watch dial and then returned it to his vest.

'By my reckoning we'll be arriving in Dodge City by eight tonight or thereabouts. The train is on time,' the attendant answered.

Stokes touched the brim of his hat. 'Much obliged.'

The attendant continued on his way and left the car. Stokes lifted his canvas bag off the floor beside his boots and placed it upon the empty seat beside the window. He opened the bag and withdrew a two-holstered gunbelt. He looped it around him and secured its buckle. He then pulled out two matched Colts.

Stokes glanced at the other passengers, then lowered his eyes and checked his weapons. After a few moments he slid them into their respective holsters. Both guns were fully loaded and ready to use as he saw fit.

He leaned slightly forward, took hold of the long leather laces that hung from the holsters and tied them around his thighs.

He was now fully armed and ready for what he knew would come when the locomotive reached its eventual destination.

Stokes leaned back and closed his

eyes as the car gently swayed from side to side. The dim lamplight that filled the car danced upon his features. Even with his eyes closed he could see every movement in the passenger car through his eyelids.

As clouds of smoke trailed past the car's windows and the locomotive gathered speed Jonas Stokes rested against the well-padded leather bench.

Yet he did not sleep.

Every sinew in his evil being was too fired-up by his eager anticipation of what was yet to occur. Stokes listened to the constant sound of the train as it advanced on his prey. Soon the iron horse would roll on into Dodge City. He gave a satisfied grunt.

Only the dead truly sleep, he thought.

Soon Ben Carter would sleep for all eternity.

4

An ominous sensde of impending danger pervaded the streets of Dodge City. All of its citizens knew that someone was due to arrive on the eight o'clock train from Yuma but none of them knew who it would be. Some speculated that there was an entire gang of merciless killers aboard the huge iron monster, coming to teach their marshal a lethal lesson. Others proclaimed that a mysterious killer was travelling to Dodge in order to take over the town.

Dodge was alive with speculation as to what the next sixty minutes might bring to the town. It was bustling with cowboys, gamblers and well-attired females. Every eye watched the tall lawman as he strode around its streets checking that all was well.

Ben Carter knew that when the church clock chimed again the train from Yuma should have arrived. He stood against a porch upright and sucked the last smoke from his cigar's twisted remains. Then he dropped it on to the sand.

His eyes flashed from beneath the wide, flat brim of his Stetson. He was studying every face that passed him as townsfolk made their habitual journeys to and from the various saloons and gambling houses that littered the long main street.

So far he had not seen any strangers.

Every sinew of his long, rangy being warned him to be aware of strangers. He realized that although Jonas Stokes was determined to kill him the outlaw would probably not attempt anything on his lonesome.

Stokes was far too wily for that, Carter reasoned.

Even the most loco of killers seldom faced their enemies without having well-paid henchmen somewhere in the shadows near by. He examined the passing faces more intently. There were no strangers in Dodge City, he thought. Not yet anyway.

A sense of relief soothed the lawman.

Ben Carter stepped down from the boardwalk and crushed the butt of his smoke beneath his boot. He slid between two tethered horses at a hitching rail and moved out into the busy street, which was crowded with various flatbed wagons and buggies travelling along its length.

The rich mingled with the less fortunate when the sun was no longer in the sky. Each night the rich emerged from their large mansions at the furthest ends of Dodge City to travel through the less affluent sections of town. They were seeking something that they could not find anywhere else.

The lawman touched his hat brim at the passing buggies and their neatly attired occupants. He knew why they were here.

When Carter reached the run-down buildings that marked the borders between each section of the town's society he paused beside a water trough and rested his black-gloved hand on its pump.

Dozens of females emerged from the shadows and started to parade down the length of the long main street. A smile spread across the marshal's troubled face. He watched as the heavily powdered women swung their small bags and swayed their bustles. They were out for business and they knew that with any luck they would be successful.

The aroma of the heavily scented women filled the street.

It drifted on the cool evening breeze. The lawman was about to continue on his way when something behind his broad shoulders alerted him.

He swung around on his boot heels and stared out into the gloom. With his left hand hovering, unaccustomed, above his gun Carter listened to the distinctive sound of an approaching stagecoach.

The six-horse team appeared from

out of the evening mist, rocking on its springs as its driver cracked a bullwhip over the heads of his team. Carter stared at the fast-moving stagecoach, its driver and shotgun guard seated on their lofty perches. Pedestrians ran out of the way of the snorting team as the vehicle moved into the main street.

Clouds of dust rose from the large rear wheels as the stagecoach slowed. Its driver pulled back on his reins and pushed his boot down upon the brake pole. The dust-covered coach slowed as it was steered towards the stagecoach office. Carter studied the vehicle and the sweating horses as they stopped expertly outside the Overland Stage-coach depot. Chains rattled like a dozen disturbed phantoms as the coach continued to rock on its springs.

Curiosity drew Ben Carter back across the busy thoroughfare towards the Overland depot. The lawman watched as the passengers slowly disembarked. Every one of them was as covered in dust as the vehicle itself.

The driver climbed down from his high seat as his guard tossed the few pieces of baggage down to their awaiting owners.

The town marshal rested one boot on the boardwalk and studied each of the passengers in turn. The driver flexed his stiff legs and then approached Carter.

The driver looked as though he had been painted in a white film of trail dust. He rubbed his face and stared at the interested lawman.

'Is anything wrong, Marshal?' he enquired. He spat a large lump of black goo at the ground. 'You look kinda troubled.'

Carter gave a shrug. He gave no other reply. He had considered the passengers and had mentally dismissed them all as suspects as they disappeared into the crowded street. There were no gunmen amongst their number. Carter lowered his boot, then touched his hat brim and walked away.

The bewildered stagecoach driver rubbed his whiskered jawline as his

guard clambered down from the stagecoach to stand beside him.

'What's wrong, Jeb?' the guard asked,
tucking the shotgun under his arm.

'There ain't nothing wrong with me
but that star-packer sure has a problem,' the driver replied.

'What kinda problem?'

'I ain't too sure, Buck,' the driver
answered. 'But something is sure eating
on that critter's craw.'

Ben Carter had barely had time to
reach the middle of the moonlit street
when two riders of daunting appearance
rode through the stagecoach dust and
thundered into the main thoroughfare.
The startled lawman stared through the
lantern light at their grim faces.

He recognized both the riders.

Carter had seen their images amongst
a stack of Wanted posters which littered
his office desk. The startled lawman lowered his left hand to the grip of his gun.

His index finger curled around the
trigger.

5

Ben Carter raced back towards his office. His boots drummed a frantic tattoo as he sped urgently onwards through the busy street at a breakneck pace. He did not trust his memory of the crude photographic likenesses on the Wanted posters upon which he had cast his eyes. He had to confirm that his supposition was correct.

Carter ran between the riders and buckboards, both moving and stationary, until he reached his office. He leapt up on to the boardwalk, grabbed the handle of his door and entered the place that he had left only ten minutes earlier. Gasping for air Carter took hold of the lamp and rested it in the centre of his desk. The exhausted lawman was about to strike a match when he saw the two horsemen pause their mounts outside the office window.

Both riders stared into the office.

The marshal straightened up as he returned their searching glare. Again his hand hovered across his belly, his fingers ready to rip the lethal .45 from its resting place.

Both horsemen stared straight at him. The intrepid lawman wondered where they would place their bullets. Would even wanted outlaws dare to shoot through his window and slay him? They showed no fear of Carter or the tin star he wore.

There was no hint of emotion on their bleak, calculating faces. They simply stared through the window of his office and held their horses in check.

A cold anger brewed inside the town marshal. With gritted teeth Carter inhaled deeply and squared up to his unwelcome observers. For the first time since he had received the telegraph message he was totally unafraid.

Even as he looked them over and saw their twin-holstered gunbelts Carter felt no fear. He could display as much defiance as he could muster, he thought.

Their cruel eyes continued to study him as if he were already in their gunsights. Carter was about to step towards the window when both horsemen jerked their reins away from the hitching rails. The horses turned and trotted away from the unlit office.

Carter moved to the window, rested a hand upon the brass rail that spanned its width and watched both riders weaving their way through the busy street. Both horsemen were heading towards the railroad station.

He looked at the horsemen long and hard, watching as they dismounted near the station building.

These were not men seeking to buy tickets. They had no intention of going anywhere. They had reached their destination and were waiting for Jonas Stokes.

Carter struck a match and touched the damp wick of his lamp. An amber glow lit up the desk and the array of papers spread untidily across its surface. He adjusted the glass funnel, lowering it over the burning wick. The office grew even brighter.

The lawman flicked through the pile of Wanted posters until he came across the pair he had been seeking. His memory had not lied to him. Carter's expression changed as he read the words printed upon both posters.

'Sam Brewer. Wanted dead or alive for murder.' Carter sighed and diverted his eyes to the second poster. 'Tom Drury. Wanted dead or alive for murder.'

Both men were valued at $200.

Carter stared up at his wall clock.

It was now twenty minutes after seven. There was now only forty minutes before the train from Yuma was due to arrive in town.

'So Jonas Stokes has hired himself a couple of gunhands,' the lawman muttered under his breath. He relit the cigar and exhaled a line of smoke. 'I ain't about to die that easy.'

6

A mile east of Dodge City dust drifted up into the moonlit heavens from the hoofs of the rider's tired mount. It hung on the frosty air as the determined rider closed the distance between the town and his lathered-up mount. There was a dragging dryness in the horseman's throat. His thirst could only be quenched by the death of two villainous souls.

Johnny Diamond did not intend to slow his pace now. Not when he had the scent of his prey filling his flared nostrils. He kept jabbing his sharp spurs into the flanks of the exhausted animal. He held the long leathers in his left hand and steered his familiar route.

Few men could ride for two days straight without rest but Diamond had done just that. He had not stopped since he had picked up the trail of the men he sought.

Men like Diamond never stopped.

They never quit.

There was only one outcome in his resolute mind. The two men he hunted would die as soon as he found their stinking hides. They were worth $200 each and that was mighty good pickings for a bounty hunter who was down to his last few silver dollars.

Diamond could not afford to stop. He had to forge on and go where the two sets of hoof tracks led him. There was no sense of doubt in his hardened mind that he would not find and kill the outlaws he sought. He would achieve his goal or die trying.

There was no black or white in his brutal world. There was just an endless, fast-flowing river of grey.

He glanced down at the dry ground and saw the imprints of two sets of hoof tracks. Diamond whipped the shoulders of his near-exhausted mount; somehow it found renewed pace.

Even the moonlight could not disguise the fact that the long-legged horse was painfully thin, just like its rider.

It had barely had time to eat or drink as its master spurred it on through the prairie that surrounded Dodge City. Its rider had had far too many other things on his fixated mind to think of nourishment.

Right now all Diamond could think about was the valuable outlaws he hunted. He needed the bounty on their heads just to survive. He needed it more than anything else.

The horseman urged his mount pitilessly up a steep rise. Clouds of choking dust enveloped the horse as its master pulled back on his reins and eased his relentless progress as he reached the flat summit of the incline.

Diamond held the weary horse in check. Steam rose from the animal and sparkled in the crisp evening air.

The moon cast its eerie light across the great plain that faced Diamond. He sat on his mount and glared down from the rise at Dodge City like a vulture awaiting the death of its next meal.

The hoof tracks led from where his horse was standing straight to the sprawling town. A satisfied smirk spread across his rugged face.

The bounty hunter sucked in air through his flared nostrils. The men he sought were now so close that he could smell them, he thought. Smell the pair of outlaws he had chased for the previous two days.

Then Diamond's eyes spotted another set of hoof tracks. The bounty hunter swung the horse to one side and stared through the moonlight at them. They were just beyond a line of sagebrush. A thought came to mind.

Who would ride within twenty feet of the two infamous outlaws? Why would anyone risk his hide to do such a dangerous thing? Before his tired mind could answer the questions he heard a noise somewhere out in the tangle of dried brush-wood.

Diamond spun his horse full circle as

a shot exploded out in the darkness. His narrowed eyes saw the shaft of red-hot lead carve its way through the evening air. He was the target the hot lead was seeking.

The survival instincts of the bounty hunter were as sure as ever. He held on to his saddle horn and dropped to the side of his tall mount. It was an old Indian trick but it still worked. He was using the horse as a shield, hanging there as the bullet passed just over the leather crown of his saddle.

Without even thinking Diamond drew one of his guns from his gunbelt. He leaned under the neck of the horse and fired at the gunsmoke.

As the clouds above his head moved across the moon the bounty hunter saw the gunman readying his rifle again. Diamond clawed back on his hammer and squeezed his trigger a second time. The man flew up into the air.

Before the gunman had hit the ground Diamond had swung back up on to his saddle and ridden across the rise to where he had seen the man land.

Diamond glared down at the wounded man. He fired another shot and sent the Winchester flying from the wounded man's hands.

He swiftly cocked his gun again and trained it on him.

'Who are you?' Diamond snarled.

'Swifty Davis,' came the muted reply.

'How come you're shooting at me?' Diamond shouted. 'Why?'

Davis forced his blood-soaked carcass off the ground and glared through unholy eyes at the gore upon his vest. He peeled the sticky fabric away from the bullet hole in his chest, then looked up at the bounty hunter atop his horse.

'Sam paid me to make sure you didn't keep trailing him and Tom,' Davis grunted, dropping his other hand down to the gun on his hip. 'I kinda made a mess of it. First my horse ran off and now I've gotten myself killed.'

Diamond kept his gun aimed on the severely wounded man below him. 'Don't go for that hogleg, Davis. I'll surely end your life if you do.'

'I'm dead anyway,' Davis said bluntly.

A thought occurred to the bounty hunter.

'Have you got bounty on your head, Davis?' Diamond enquired casually. 'Are you worth any money?'

Davis's fingers flexed over the holstered grip of his gun.

'Nope, I ain't. I'm not on any Wanted posters.' Davis coughed as blood poured from his wound.

'That's a crying shame.' The bounty hunter spat. 'I sure hate wasting good bullets on worthless varmints like you.'

Davis drew his gun. Before he was able to raise and aim the .45 a deafening shot lit up the distance between the two men. Davis crashed back on to the ground. Smoke rose from the hole in the centre of his temple.

Diamond shook his head.

'Damn it all. There ain't no profit in killing back-shooters.' The bounty hunter reloaded his weapon and pushed it back into its holster. He straightened up and gathered his reins together.

Diamond eased himself up in his stirrups and looped his right leg over the cantle. In one fluid movement the bounty hunter dismounted and studied the terrain that lay ahead of him. He reached to his saddlebags and unbuckled his satchel. He lifted its leather flap, pulled out a bag and spread its contents on the ground in front of the sweating horse.

The hungry horse dropped its head and gratefully started to eat the grain as its master returned the bag. Diamond looped the thin ribbon of leather through its buckle and turned to look again over the landscape.

His eyes were stinging with weariness. Diamond rubbed them with the long tails of his bandanna.

Whilst the horse ate its meagre meal the bounty hunter stared blankly at the town that lay below. He studied it carefully. Not one thing was missed by his eagle-eyed observance.

Diamond could see the moonlit railtracks. They gleamed like silver in the eerie light of the full moon. His eyes drifted to the west of the town where a few hundred steers waited to be boarded upon the next stock train and sent East.

Their lives were nearly over, he thought.

Just like the two men he hunted.

Diamond thrust his hand into his pocket.

He searched for and found the pair of crumpled Wanted posters buried deep in the pocket. He shook them loose and stared at the two images printed upon them. The bounty hunter had no way of knowing it but in his hand he held prints of the very same posters that Marshal Carter was looking at in his office.

He glared as only a hunter could glare at the crude pictures of Sam Brewer and Tom Drury. They were worth $200 each, dead or alive. It was a fortune to a man who had barely three silver dollars to his name.

'You're dead men just like your pal Davis here,' Diamond murmured. He chuckled as he glanced at the blood-covered body near him, then returned his attention to the town. 'You just don't know it yet.'

He gave a slow, knowing nod and returned the papers to his deep pocket. Once more Diamond studied the land that surrounded him. There were no further signs of life.

His eyes drifted back to the glittering town below him. A cruel smile stretched across his hardened features as he thought about the outlaws.

'You don't know it, boys, but Johnny Diamond is coming to collect the bounty on your stinking heads.' He smirked, grabbed his saddle horn, poked his boot into the stirrup and raised himself up on to his saddle. Dodge City was a large town compared to many but Diamond had hunted his prey in far larger places.

Not one of the outlaws he had hunted over the years had ever managed to escape from him. He sniffed at the air like a human bloodhound. He had their scent in his nostrils. Soon he would have their bodies in his gunsights.

He gathered his reins up in his hands and pulled on the long leathers.

The horse raised its head.

Diamond spurred.

7

An array of buildings stood flanking both sides of the railroad tracks in Dodge City. The rails gleamed as evidence of the traffic of trains that had constantly polished them. Beyond the buildings opposite the ticket office lay large, empty stock pens, which stretched over several acres. Their weathered poles glinted in the moonlight and awaited the next herd of longhorns or white-faced steers coming to fill them in readiness for transporting back East. This night, however, was different: the only thing expected was a passenger train from Yuma with its cargo of the demented Jonas Stokes aboard.

Every tick of the station clock brought that train closer as it thundered across the plains. The two outlaws who waited for the arrival of the train might have been worth the same amount of money on their Wanted posters but otherwise they could not have been more different.

One was seasoned and had acquired long ago the ability to relax and wait patiently, whilst the other was younger and more anxious.

Sam Brewer rested one boot on a bench and stared in through the arched ticket-office window at the stationmaster within. The outlaw was well aware that the aged stationmaster knew that he was being observed, yet the man showed no interest. Brewer pulled out a long thin cigar, bit off its tip and rammed it into his mouth. He leaned down and scratched a match along the boards of the bench, then cupped the flame in his gloved hands.

If Sam Brewer had any nervous doubts about the outcome of their latest venture, they did not show. He remained calm as a cloud of smoke drifted around his head.

Like so many in his sordid profession he was confident in his own abilities.

He sucked the toxic smoke deep into his lungs and turned his head. He silently watched his nervous partner. Tom Drury had ventured to the very edge of the long platform and was looking out at the moonlit tracks. Brewer observed that Drury was pounding his holstered guns with clenched fists and he sighed.

The younger outlaw was scared. So utterly scared that he could not stand still even for a few seconds, Brewer thought. Men like Drury tended not to live as long as most. They allowed every shadow to whittle away at their souls until nothing remained. Brewer had seen fear cause so many young hotheads to make grave mistakes.

After a few moments Drury marched back to where Brewer stood smoking his cigar.

'Where the hell is the damn train, Sam?' Drury ranted. 'Where in tarnation is Stokes?'

Brewer looked calmly at his cohort.

'Quit fretting, Tom,' he advised, chewing on his cigar. 'We got here early. Jonas's train ain't due until eight.'

Drury ran a hand over his neck anxiously. 'What's the time now?' he asked.

Brewer shrugged. 'How should I know? I don't own a timepiece. All I know for sure is that the eight o'clock train from Yuma ain't arrived yet, so it can't be eight.'

The less experienced Drury walked to the tracks, then returned to his partner. 'That don't make no sense at all, Sam. What if the train's late?'

Brewer grabbed his partner's shoulder and hauled him backwards until he landed on the bench. He then pointed his smoking cigar at Drury.

'Easy, Tom. You're fretting like an old lady. We've bin hired to help Jonas and we're here. No call for fretting. All we gotta do is wait until that iron horse shows. Savvy?'

Drury leaned forward. He rested his

elbows on his thighs and rocked as if a million ants had crawled into his long johns.

'I just don't cotton to that marshal recognizing us before Stokes has had time to plug the varmint, Sam,' he explained. 'And what if Stokes gets himself killed? That lawman will come gunning after us.'

Sam Brewer exhaled a cloud of smoke.

'You're plumb irritating when you ain't had any liquor, Tom,' Brewer complained, producing another cigar from his trail-coat pocket. 'Here. Suck on this weed and quit worrying. By the time you've smoked this cigar Jonas will be here.'

The younger outlaw shook his head and pushed the cigar away from him as though it contained poison.

'You know I don't smoke, Sam,' Drury snapped. 'Them things ain't good for you.'

'They're a heap better than chewing on lead,' Brewer remarked, and slid the cigar back into his pocket. 'Think on that.'

Drury cast his eyes on the frustrated outlaw. 'Think on what?'

Brewer looked at the heavens and shook a fist at the stars. 'Give me strength, Lord. Why'd you have to burden me with a non-smoking worry-wart for a partner?'

Suddenly both men heard the distant sound of a train's whistle cut through the frosty air. Both their heads turned at the same moment.

'Did you hear that, Sam?' Drury asked.

'I ain't deaf,' Brewer replied.

Drury stood. 'It's coming. It's finally coming, Sam.'

Sam Brewer blew the ash from his cigar and raised an eyebrow. He sat down and stared as his cohort watched the railtracks for a train which he himself knew would still take at least twenty minutes to reach Dodge City.

'Take it easy, Tom. We still got plenty of time before that train gets here,'

Brewer told the youngster as Drury beat his guns with clenched fists again.

His assurance did nothing to calm his excited partner down so Brewer returned his cigar to his lips and sucked hard.

'Keep them eyes peeled, Tom.'

'I surely will,' Drury naïvely said.

Brewer shook his head and pulled down the brim of his Stetson. He closed his eyes and would not reopen them until he heard the train hissing steam.

8

Marshal Ben Carter had also heard the train whistling out on the prairie. It was a warning that even he could not deny. A sudden urgency gripped the lawman. He knew that to take on Jonas Stokes and his hired henchmen alone was probably more than most able-bodied men could do. For a man with a useless claw instead of a gun hand, it was probably suicidal.

Carter had finally resolved to swallow his pride and try to find help. Yet, as he left his office he knew that seeking help might be lot harder than he hoped. He strode down the centre of the street, glancing to his left and right in turn. So many saloons filled with so many men, he thought. Were there any men in Dodge City willing to risk their lives and help him?

With each step of his long legs the

brutal truth dawned upon the troubled lawman. Not one of the townspeople of Dodge had ever shown their elected law officer anything but contempt.

That was his own fault. He moved between half a dozen horses at a hitching rail and stepped up on to the boardwalk of the Long Branch saloon.

He moved towards its swing doors and looked over them into the heart of the busy saloon. The tobacco smoke inside was thick enough to cut with a sabre. At least sixty men mingled with a handful of bar girls.

The marshal lowered his head and pushed the swing doors apart. He had barely taken two steps when the saloon fell into total silence.

A chill traced his backbone.

Every eye in the Long Branch watched the lawman as he slowly made his way across the sawdust-covered floor towards the bar counter. The lawman felt as though he were a walking dead man as he continued. Every customer and bar girl stepped aside as if he had smallpox and they were afraid that they might catch it.

He reached the bar, placed his boot upon its brass rail and rested his gloved right hand upon the damp counter. He looked up at the bartender and nodded.

'Howdy, Shiloh,' Carter said.

'Howdy, Marshal.' The bartender returned the greeting and continued drying glasses. 'You want a drink?'

It was against every rule Carter had set himself but now he realized that since he had become town marshal things had changed.

'Yeah, I'll have a beer,' Carter answered.

A hushed gasp filled the room. No one had ever seen Carter drinking anything stronger than coffee before. For the first time he was showing them that he was human after all.

'A beer it'll be.' Shiloh Watkins nodded in shock as he moved to the barrel on the top of his counter and placed a glass beneath its tap.

Carter pulled a coin from his vest

pocket and placed it down at the same moment as his beer arrived. The lawman raised his left hand and lifted the glass to his lips. He drank the entire contents in one go.

'Same again,' Carter muttered, pushing his empty glass forward.

The bartender gave a nod. 'Same again it'll be.'

Carter turned and glanced around the faces that stared at him. There still was not a hint of emotion upon his chiselled features.

'You all seem to know that there's a critter coming to Dodge,' Carter said. 'You also might know why he's coming here.'

'To kill you, Marshal,' a brave voice said from deep in the crowd. The lawman gave a nod.

Carter smiled. 'Yep. That's exactly right. The critter is coming to kill me and I need some help.'

The admission caused another gasp to fill the saloon. It was the first time that any of them could remember hearing Carter admit his own mortality.

The lawman pushed the brim of his hat back until it rested on the crown of his head.

'I'm looking for help,' Carter repeated. 'I'm looking for deputies.'

A stunned silence filled the Long Branch. None of the saloon's patrons could believe what they had heard. There was no hint of any response from any of them.

Carter lifted his beer and took another sip. He lowered it and looked around the saloon.

'No takers?' he asked.

Once more the crowd remained silent.

Carter finished his beer and placed the empty glass down upon the bar counter. He sighed, rubbed his mouth along his sleeve and walked away from the bar.

'Much obliged,' Carter said.

They watched the lawman make his way towards the swing doors and push his way back into Front Street. Carter paused when he reached the boardwalk and looked out into the street. Then he heard noise breaking out inside the Long Branch.

The lawman stepped down into the street and started walking. There was no destination. He just walked. Carter wondered if there was any point in seeking help anywhere else in town.

He knew he would receive the same silence wherever he went in Dodge. Carter slid his hand into his pocket and pulled out the last of his cigars.

As he walked he pushed the cigar in the corner of his mouth. He hoped that he had enough time to finish it.

He lit the fresh cigar and looked up at the church clock.

It was ten minutes before eight. In the distance he could hear the eerie sound of the train whistle blowing again. The driver was alerting the station-master that he was close, Carter thought. The huge locomotive was nearing Dodge bringing with it the creature who had vowed to destroy Ben Carter.

Carter glanced at the church clock once again.

There was little time left. The only thing the marshal could do was await his fate.

9

It was as though an iron monster spitting steam and red-hot cinders was approaching Dodge City. No creature from legendary fables could have appeared more daunting to the unaware. The great black steam locomotive swayed as it negotiated the tracks towards the long platform and its array of wooden buildings. The driver pulled on his cord as he leaned out from his cab. Each tug sent a deafening sound out from the locomotive's whistle.

The steam train was slowing as it approached. Its wheels were sending out sparks on either side of the tracks as they slowly responded. The driver and engineer were carefully braking and their gigantic charge was obeying their commands.

In the moonlight the locomotive

made an awesome vision. It was a majestic sight that, once seen, was never forgotten.

The passengers in the first car rose to their feet and collected their belongings together. They had been alerted by the attendant as he strolled through each car in turn that they were due to arrive in Dodge City only five minutes late.

Jonas Stokes was standing. He held his canvas bag in his hand as the train slowed on its approach to the station. The lights of Dodge City were a welcome difference from the vast, moonlit desert he had travelled through to reach the sprawling settlement.

Yet Stokes did not move. He simply watched.

The sound of the wheels as they went over the rail joints filled the car as men and women prepared for their imminent arrival in Dodge.

The car was filled with the laughter of those who knew they had arrived home safely. They moved along the railway car in good order. Stokes remained standing, watching his fellow travellers.

He did not smile.

He just continued to watch.

No bird of prey could have watched with more intensity or with such evil as festered in his rancid soul. Stokes was a creature who watched long and hard before he struck. Three years in prison had not changed that one bit. It had only increased his desire to continue where he had left off.

His eyes flashed to the line of windows. The train was barely moving as it rolled into the station. The other men and women held on to the tops of the seats as they ventured along towards the door at the end of the car.

Jonas Stokes just balanced like a tightrope walker. His body adjusted with each movement of the rocking train.

Then he saw his two henchmen on the platform.

Brewer and Drury rose to their feet

from the bench when they spotted him through the windows of the car. Jonas Stokes started to walk between the rows of seats as the locomotive came to a sudden halt.

Everyone in the car took a backward step before they were able to continue. Stokes alone remained perfectly balanced. The passengers proceeded out of the well-lit car, stepping down from the train into the moonlight. Only the lights from inside the ticket office and the waiting rooms splashed on to the disembarking passengers.

Brewer and Drury stood with their hands resting on their holstered guns. They studied every face but the preoccupied passengers passed by the two deadly outlaws without even noticing them.

Stokes was the last of the train's passengers to step down from the train. He did not look at the two men who awaited him as he approached.

He knew where they were and moved towards them.

The deadly gunman placed his canvas bag on the bench beside his men and removed his tie. He folded it carefully and dropped it into the bag. Stokes secured the bag's fastener and straightened up.

He turned and looked at Sam Brewer and Tom Drury.

'You got my message then, Sam,' Stokes said drily. His eyes surveyed the unfamiliar Drury. 'Who's this varmint? I don't recall ever setting eyes upon him before.'

'You're right, Jonas. This is Tom Drury,' Brewer answered. 'We've been riding together for the last two years.'

Stokes eyed Drury, then turned to Brewer and spoke as though the younger outlaw was not within earshot.

'Is he any good, Sam?' Stokes asked. 'He sure sweats a lot.'

Brewer nodded. 'He's a good gun, Jonas. Real good.'

Stokes loosened his stiff collar and removed its stud.

'That's fine. Mighty fine,' he said.

'The last thing I need is a critter that I can't trust.'

Drury bit his lower lip. 'I'm honoured to be working with you, Mr Stokes. I'll not let you down.'

Stokes glanced at the young outlaw. 'I'll hold you to that, Drury. You best remember that. I'm a mean critter when riled.'

Brewer and Drury watched as Stokes pushed the tails of his coat over his gun grips. The old outlaw then looked at both his hired guns with an icy stare that demanded the truth.

'Have either of you seen Carter?' he asked them.

They both nodded.

'We seen him in his office just after we rode into town, Jonas.' Brewer grinned. 'He sure looked old. I've never seen a lawman that looks as old as Carter does.'

Stokes nodded.

'He'll not get any older, Sam. I promise you that.'

The two outlaws laughed as Stokes

leaned into the arched window of the ticket office. The stationmaster ventured towards the window and stared at the unsmiling face.

'Can I help you, mister?' he asked.

Stokes lifted his bag and handed it through the window.

'Keep this bag safe. I'll be back.'

'We don't do that,' the stationmaster told Stokes.

Stokes smiled. Then he drew and cocked one of his guns. He aimed the .45 at the face of the older man.

'I didn't hear you, friend. Say that again.'

The stationmaster accepted the canvas bag. He was trembling as he spoke.

'I said that it'll be a pleasure, mister.'

Stokes holstered his weapon and glanced at his men.

'C'mon. We got a lawman to skin.'

10

Ben Carter had heard the train whistle as he reached the café opposite his office. A chill overwhelmed the lawman. He knew that if the telegraph message he had received two hours earlier was correct Jonas Stokes had arrived. That thought made the lawman anxious. He noticed that the men and women who had filled the street were now rushing away in droves.

The marshal watched as buggies swung around and sped away from the heart of Dodge. The rich suddenly lost all interest in the powdered ladies and headed for their homes. Buckboards were whipped and driven out of town at even greater speed.

Within a matter of seconds Carter found himself quite alone in the middle of Dodge. The crowds had vanished without trace.

One by one he heard doors locking and lanterns being extinguished. Darkness fell in store after store.

Carter remained perfectly still. His mind raced as he stared around the empty street. Apart from tethered horses only the marshal remained out in the open. He stepped down from the boardwalk and moved back through the moonlight in the direction of his office. He was dumbfounded by the sudden change.

He knew why the townspeople had fled. There was no mystery. The rumour that an avenging killer was returning to kill the marshal had come true. Now Carter imagined that the onlookers had suddenly realized that once *he* was dead Stokes might choose to keep on fanning his gun hammer.

They did not wish to join their marshal in the funeral parlour.

Halfway across the street he heard the pounding of a horse's hoofs. The lawman swung on his boot leather. For a moment he could see nothing through the frosty air. Then a spine-chilling vision emerged a few hundred yards away.

It was like staring at a ghost suddenly materializing before him. Caked in two days of trail dust both horse and rider looked more dead than alive to the lawman. Carter swallowed hard as he watched the unholy apparition ride steadily towards him.

The lean horseman guided his mount with one hand whilst his other rested upon the grip of a holstered gun.

This was no ghost, Carter thought.

Whoever this horseman was he was real.

Carter rested his own hand on his own holstered gun. His unblinking eyes remained fixed upon the horseman. He inhaled on his cigar and squared up to the rider.

Johnny Diamond narrowed his eyes and saw the tin star glinting in the light of the street lanterns. He aimed his beleaguered mount towards the defiant lawman.

Carter stood his ground and drew his gun. As Diamond covered the two hundred yards between them the lawman remained facing him.

Diamond allowed his horse to ride right up to the stationary figure but still Carter did not flinch. At the very last moment the bounty hunter dragged his reins back and stopped his charge only a few feet from the lawman.

Each man stared at the other.

They were weighing each other up.

'Who the hell are you, stranger?' Carter snarled, returning his gun to its holster.

Johnny Diamond dismounted and led his horse towards the nearest water trough. He looped his reins over the hitching rail and secured his leathers firmly.

'The name's Diamond, Marshal,' he muttered, then faced the lawman. 'Johnny Diamond.'

Carter moved towards the man. 'I've heard the name.'

'I'm a bounty hunter, Marshal,'

Diamond added. 'A scum-sucking bounty hunter.'

The lawman chuckled.

'Is that what folks call you?' he asked.

'Yep.' Diamond shrugged. 'They call me a lot worse as well. What they call you?'

'Ben Carter.' Carter moved around the tall, thin figure and studied him in detail. He then paused and rubbed his chin. 'Reckon most folks don't cotton to critters like you, Diamond. They want the outlaws rounded up and killed but they ain't got the stomach for the varmints that do their dirty work for them.'

Diamond tilted his head. 'Reckon you're a smart old man, Marshal. I don't meet many of your breed too often.'

Carter, still fearful about the threatening telegram, looked over his shoulder at the church clock. The lawman rubbed the sweat from his brow and sighed heavily.

'Is something bothering you, Marshal?' Diamond asked. He produced a cigar from his inside pocket, bit off its tip and placed it between his teeth. 'You look kinda fretful, old-timer.'

It was now exactly two minutes after eight. The bounty hunter was quite right. Carter was fretful. He could not hide the concern in his face.

Carter nodded slowly. 'You're dead right, Diamond. I am troubled. The Yuma train arrived a short while back. There's a varmint on that train who reckons he's gonna kill me. Not that you'd be interested.'

Diamond struck a match with his thumbnail and raised it to his cigar. He sucked in the strong smoke and blew out the flickering flame. Then he eased himself next to the troubled lawman.

'If he's got two varmints with him called Brewer and Drury I'm mighty interested, Marshal,' the bounty hunter said through a line of smoke.

Carter raised both eyebrows.

'Are they the critters you're after?' he asked.

Diamond nodded. 'Yep. They sure are.'

Ben Carter moved closer to the thin bounty hunter.

'I've got a proposition for you, Diamond,' the sheriff told him. 'One which might make you a whole lot more money than the four hundred dollars Brewer and Drury will bring you.'

Johnny Diamond studied the lawman carefully. A wry smile broke across his features. He adjusted his Stetson and tilted his head.

'More money than Brewer and Drury are worth?'

Carter nodded firmly. 'A lot more money.'

'I'm listening, Marshal.' The bounty hunter nodded. 'Spill your proposition.'

The lawman looked around the empty street.

'First we'd best get off the street, Diamond,' Carter suggested. 'I'd hate for us to eat lead before I get a chance to explain. C'mon.'

The bounty hunter trailed the marshal as Carter led him to the relative safety of the shadows.

11

Jonas Stokes led Brewer and Drury away from the rail station as the big locomotive snorted steam behind them. The wheels spun and then gripped the tracks as the mighty engine moved away from the platform. The whistle sounded and slowly the entire train pulled out of Dodge City.

The three deadly killers slipped through the shadows and walked into the moonlight. Stokes paused as his eyes checked out the town that faced them. The large, bright moon lit up the roof-tops of the buildings as the evil avenger tried to recall every nook and cranny. Three years was a long time and he knew things might have changed, but everything appeared to be as he recalled it.

Stokes pointed to his cohorts' mounts.

'I want you boys to circle the town and come in from the south,' he instructed. 'I want that stinking starpacker to get caught in the middle. I want him running scared as we close in on the varmint.'

Sam Brewer stared to where Stokes was looking. 'The town sure is big, Jonas. Bigger than I expected. That marshal could hide in a hundred different holes there.'

Stokes gave a contemptuous grunt.

'Carter will have to take a stagecoach to Hell before he finds a hole big enough to crawl into, Sam.'

Brewer untied his mount and threw himself up on to the back of his saddle. Drury copied his partner's actions as Stokes continued down the rise into the very soul of Dodge City.

Brewer and his cohort had received their instructions and neither was brave enough to disobey. They dared not argue with their leader. Stokes was their paymaster and until the job was completed, he called the shots.

The two riders spurred their mounts and rode in different directions.

Brewer rode to the left as Drury headed right. Neither outlaw was going to ride into the main thoroughfare of Dodge, but rather skirt around the town's centre.

Dust rose into the night air as the horsemen galloped away from the station whilst Stokes continued straight on into the heart of town.

As Stokes stretched his legs he kept his hands on his gun grips. He had no intension of giving the lawman a fair chance of beating him on the draw.

Jonas Stokes intended to win this fight.

Carter had to die the death of a thousand cuts.

In less than five minutes Dodge City had become chillingly silent. When the train from Yuma had pulled into the station every living soul in the town knew that Stokes had arrived.

Few of those who lived in the busy cowtown could remember the drunken outlaw whom their marshal had got the better of three years before, but they knew why he had returned.

Pride.

Stokes had returned for only one purpose.

He intended torturing and killing their marshal because his precious pride had been damaged. Stokes had imagined that men, women and children had laughed at him when he was shackled and driven off like an animal in a barred cage.

Ben Carter had to be taught a lesson. He had to be taught that no one ever made Jonas Stokes look foolish and lived to brag about it.

Every saloon had dozens of faces pressed up against its window and many more looking over the tops of their swing doors.

For hours the people of Dodge had anticipated witnessing a killing, but now, as the train blasted its high-pitched whistle and left the town, they started to doubt their wisdom.

None of them cared to get caught in the cross-fire of a real shoot-out. They had eagerly wanted to see death but did not want to end up dead themselves.

No matter how much they despised Ben Carter, they began to realize that when he was dead there would be no law in their settlement.

Without law they were defenceless.

What had seemed only two hours earlier to be nothing more than a chance to see an execution was no longer quite so exciting to any of them. They were no longer smiling as they huddled together behind their locked doors.

Now they cowered like the vermin they truly were.

A gasp of terror filled the Long Branch saloon as its customers caught sight of the determined Stokes heading down the slope from the railroad. They pulled its double doors shut and bolted them.

As he reached the centre of Front Street the sound of more doors being slammed and bolted could be heard.

Stokes strode into the street, his hands gripping his holstered guns. His eyes searched for any sign of his intended victim.

'I'm here, Carter,' Stokes bellowed. 'Where are you? Are you hiding like the chicken-livered varmint we both know you are?'

The words echoed off the false fronts that lined the long street. There was no reply from the lawman. Stokes continued to walk on defiantly.

'Where the hell are you? I figured on you being a whole lot braver than this, Carter,' Stokes yelled out as he paused and studied the street. Every store, saloon, gambling hall and whorehouse was shuttered. Only the street lanterns cast any light from their high poles. Their amber glow lit up the street. 'Where are you?'

Still there was no reply.

His words bounced off the walls that flanked him.

Stokes was getting angrier with every

stride. He was furious that the lawman he had travelled from Yuma to kill was hiding. Stokes moved past the large livery stable, which towered over all the other buildings, apart from the church tower.

Stokes moved between their shadows as he hunted his elusive prey.

Stokes drew both his guns and eased their hammers back until they fully locked. His gaze darted along every building in the street as he searched vainly for Carter.

Where was the lawman?

Where was Ben Carter?

A fiery rage smouldered inside Stokes. He wanted to kill the marshal more than anything else. Revenge was eating at the innards of the desperate killer like a ravenous cancer which could not be stopped.

Stokes looked along the deserted street.

Then he observed the faces of the town's apprehensive citizens. They were watching him. Stokes lowered his head and turned to face the Long Branch saloon.

His face wore a cruel smile as he raised both weapons and aimed them at the saloon. The people who were watching him from there disappeared as they saw the moonlight glinting on the barrels of his deadly weaponry.

Stokes walked towards the saloon. There was purpose in every step.

He had entered Dodge City with a plan.

Now he had decided to change it.

12

There was an unusual silence in Front Street. It was only broken when the deadly gunman stepped up on to the boardwalk outside the locked doors of the saloon. The weathered boards creaked as Jonas Stokes stepped closer and aimed his guns at the lock.

The entire street rocked as Stokes pulled back on his triggers. Two deafening shafts of lightning spewed from the barrels and shattered the lock. It exploded and fell in fragments on to the boardwalk.

With venomous fury Stokes raised his right leg and kicked at what was left of the lock. The remains of the bolt flew off the splintered woodwork.

To the horror of those inside the saloon the double doors were torn from their hinges and crashed inward. The customers barely had time to hit the sawdust-covered floorboards before Stokes entered.

Even in the darkness of the saloon Stokes could see the whites of their eyes. The killer stood like a statue with his smoking weaponry in his hands.

'Where's the marshal?' he yelled out.

'Marshal Carter ain't in here,' a voice screamed out.

Jonas Stokes stared with cold eyes around the room full of shaking people. His thumbs cocked both guns again.

'I ain't looking for Carter in here,' he observed drily.

'Then what do you want?' another of the terrified people asked from the gloom.

Amused by the terror he was still capable of arousing in innocent people, Stokes walked to the bar counter and turned around. His back was propped against the damp mahogany.

'What do I want? I want a bunch of victims,' he drawled callously. 'I need me a whole herd of people to shoot.'

A horrified gasp filled the saloon.

Stokes ignored it and stepped closer to the men and women gathered in the black depths of the shadows.

'Why?' a female voice cried out.

'We ain't done nothing,' another yelled. 'Why do you wanna kill us? Why?'

Stokes held his guns in his hands and smiled at the naïve question.

'Why?' He repeated the question, then added, 'I'll tell you why. I need that yellow-spined marshal to crawl out from whatever rock he's hiding under and come when he's called. I sure don't like being made to wait.'

There was a long, chilling silence, then Stokes started to speak again.

'By my reckoning the only way I can get Marshal Carter to show himself is to start killing folks.' Stokes lowered his head and then added ominously, 'I've chosen you to do the dying.'

Before the crowd had time to absorb his words Stokes turned his guns to one side and fired them both. White flashes lit up the darkness as he sent two lethal bullets into the mass of cowering townspeople.

The saloon vibrated to the sound of two bodies lifelessly hitting the floor.

Panic erupted like a volcano.

The common belief is that only women scream but Stokes proved that theory to be wrong. Both men and women screamed hysterically as they stampeded towards the shattered doorway.

Jonas Stokes watched them running for their lives.

He cocked his hammers again and fired two more deafening shots after them. He did not miss either of his targets. As two men arched and fell across the boardwalk the killer started to laugh. Stokes continued to pick the fleeing saloon patrons off at will.

Again he laughed as smoke billowed from his hot barrels.

It was not the laughter of a sane man.

13

Johnny Diamond moved next to the kneeling marshal and rested a hand upon his broad shoulder. He stared through the moonlight down along the street to where they could both see and hear the massacre of innocent souls. Each man stared in disbelief as men fell wounded or dead as they tried to flee the Long Branch saloon. The only ones to manage to escape the deadly bullets of Stokes were those who happened to run from the saloon when Stokes was forced to reload.

They watched in awe as men and females scrambled for their very lives over the bodies of the dead. It was a gut-churning sight even for men who had lived their lives in the brutal West.

'Who in tarnation is doing all that killing?' Diamond asked his companion. 'Brewer and Drury ain't known for shooting folks in the back.'

Carter rose to his full height. 'It's not the critters you're hunting, Diamond.'

'Then who is doing all that shooting?' The bounty hunter looked perplexed. He had hunted the lowest kind of man in his time but none of them had slaughtered innocent men and women by shooting them in the back.

'Jonas Stokes.' Carter spat the name as though it were poison. 'I reckon it's about time I showed myself and faced the music.'

Diamond gripped the lawman's sleeve.

'I don't reckon you'd last any longer than them poor critters if you got brave, Marshal,' Diamond observed. He pointed at the pile of bodies.

'What do you mean, Diamond?'

The bounty hunter grabbed hold of Carter's right hand and raised it up until it was under his nose. He looked at the black glove and then back into the town marshal's eyes. Carter tugged his hand free.

Diamond shook his head.

'You're either mighty brave or you're just plumb loco, Carter,' he said. 'If you try to take on a gunfighter like Stokes then you're just suicidal. Which is it, friend?'

Carter turned away from the bounty hunter.

'I don't know what you're gabbing about,' he lied.

'I reckon you do.' Diamond bit his lip. 'How long have you been hiding that claw and pretending it's a hand? How long have you been bluffing the town's folks that this is a real working hand?'

The marshal felt as though a mighty weight had been lifted from his broad shoulders. At last someone else knew the secret that had tormented him for far too long. He lowered his head.

'Well?' Diamond repeated as he demanded an answer. 'How long have you had a practically useless hand, Marshal?'

Carter turned and stared through the

eerie moonlight at the bounty hunter's face. He shrugged.

'For a few years,' he admitted. 'When did you notice?'

Diamond pulled out a long, thin cigar from his pocket, bit off its tip and spat it at the ground.

'I noticed it when I first rode into town a while back.' The bounty hunter was about to strike a match when he spotted a rider pass behind a building opposite them. He removed the long weed from his lips and pushed it into the marshal's mouth. 'Chew on that awhile, old-timer. I've got me some bounty to collect.'

Carter pulled the cigar from his lips and watched as the bounty hunter ran across the street and vanished from view. Then he heard the sound of a horse snorting behind him as it too approached through the shadows. Carter turned round, narrowed his eyes and clumsily drew his gun.

Then the lawman realized that there was another horse. This one was moving behind the building he was using for cover, Carter told himself.

Slowly but fearlessly the lawman moved towards the sound.

14

Behind the façades of Front Street was a maze of alleyways filled with the stench of outhouses and discarded garbage. Tom Drury eased back on his reins as he reached the last of the town's wooden buildings and lifted the tails of his bandanna to mop his face. Drury felt the salt of his sweat burning into his eyes like red-hot branding-irons.

He had heard movement but could not work out where or what it was. Drury put his weight on to his left stirrup and leaned from his saddle. He saw nothing, and that made the outlaw nervous. Drury hauled himself back on to his saddle and steadied himself.

The outlaw had been unnerved by the sound of gunfire out in the street. That had not been in Stokes's original plan, he thought. The wanted man swung his mount around and aimed its nose at the gap between two buildings. He was about to spur his horse forward when suddenly he heard something above him.

It was the same noise as he had heard a few moments before. Spurs were jangling from above him.

Drury stopped his mount and leaned back in his saddle. His sore eyes vainly searched the balcony. The sound grew louder. Suddenly Drury saw a black mass hurtling down towards him. The bounty hunter proved his agility and climbed up to the balcony of one of the structures. Diamond then raced down the length of the veranda until he reached its end, from where he propelled himself off the railings.

With his long trail coat spread out he flew through the air like a dropping, outspread flag.

Startled, Drury barely had time to see the bounty hunter when Diamond caught the outlaw around the shoulders with wide-open arms. The sheer force of the impact sent both men toppling over the bounty hunter's saddle cantle.

Both men crashed into the ground as the terrified horse bucked and then galloped through the alleyway.

The bounty hunter was first to his feet. He reached down, hauled Drury up by his bandanna and punched him powerfully in the jaw.

The sound of cracking teeth filled the alley as Drury's head was knocked backwards. The stunned outlaw crashed to the ground. Diamond hovered above him, like a ravenous wolf about to tear its prey apart.

Diamond stared down at the blood-covered face. The light of the moon made Drury's face appear even more hideous. The bounty hunter clenched his fist and was about to deliver some further blows when Drury opened his eyes again.

'Who are you?' the outlaw spat, blood streaming from both sides of his mouth.

'I'm your executioner, Drury,' Diamond snarled.

The bounty hunter leaned down and grabbed the outlaw again. This time the dazed youngster had enough wits about him to raise a leg and kick Diamond in the belt buckle.

This time it was Johnny Diamond who went crashing to the ground. Drury rolled over and then forced himself up on to his feet.

He swayed like a drunkard and blinked hard. Drury spat blood at the ground and staggered towards Diamond. He swung a boot into the ribs of the winded bounty hunter. Diamond gasped as he buckled and wrapped around the pointed boot.

Mustering every scrap of his strength Diamond grabbed the boot and twisted it. The outlaw moved backwards into the wooden fencing. Drury did not fall, though. He refused to fall.

Drury charged like a raging bull at his injured foe. He leapt on top of the winded Diamond. With clenched fists he landed a left and a right punch into the bounty hunter's jaw.

There was no response so the youngster continued to batter his opponent mercilessly.

Diamond felt his head rocking under the barrage of punches before he managed to force his left arm up. He grabbed Drury by the throat and sank his long fingers into the outlaw's flesh.

Diamond squeezed at Drury's throat. The choking man gasped as he reached up to the hand that was throttling the very life from him.

As Diamond maintained his deadly grip he smashed a fist into the belly of the man above him. Drury buckled as a second blow caught the side of his head.

Diamond pushed Drury off him and leapt to his feet.

Blood was trailing from the corners of his eyes as the bounty hunter stood above the outlaw. Diamond snarled at the outlaw on the ground and panted.

'I'll give you one thing, kid,' Diamond gasped. 'You sure put up a mighty good fight and no mistake.'

Tom Drury did not utter a word at first. He simply lowered his hands from his bruised throat and glared at the towering bounty hunter. His arms continued to move down his supine body until his hands hovered above his gun grips.

'I'm gonna kill you,' Drury croaked.

'I'd not try if I was you,' Diamond warned his combatant. Then he saw the glinting of a drawn .45 catch the moonlight as its barrel was aimed straight up at him. The bounty hunter jumped sideways as Drury squeezed its trigger.

The alley resounded as the deafening shot ripped through the tails of his long trail coat.

Diamond felt the bullet's heat as it narrowly missed him.

Faster than most people could blink Johnny Diamond drew one of his own guns. He fanned its hammer again and again, sending fiery rods of lethal venom down into Drury. The bounty hunter quit when only smoke trailed from his six-shooter.

Diamond watched as the outlaw's arm fell limply to his side as life raced from his bullet-ridden body. Drury seemed to deflate as air escaped from the numerous bullet holes in his blood-soaked chest. The bounty hunter stepped over the lifeless corpse, kicked the gun from the dead hand and surveyed his handiwork.

The blood gleamed in the moonlight.

Smoke rose from the bullet holes.

With the shots still echoing in his ears, Johnny Diamond swiftly reloaded his smoking weapon and returned to the shadows.

15

The lawman cautiously edged through the darkness. The sound of the horse still lured Carter deeper into the shadows. He gripped his gun in his left hand and looked all about him as he tried to work out where the horseman was. After he had ventured more than a hundred yards away from Front Street he stopped to get his bearings.

Each fenced wall was just high enough to keep prying eyes from looking over them. Carter held his gun and looked both to his left and right. High walls guarded the premises of all the larger buildings of Front Street.

Carter felt his shirt clinging to his sweating back as he moved even deeper into the blackness. The moon had not yet managed to rise high enough into the cloudless sky to cast its eerie illumination into the narrow alleys. All was in shadow.

The horseman might be anywhere. Carter moved his gun from side to side. If Stokes's mysterious henchman showed himself, the lawman told himself, he would try to shoot him. Yet he knew that would not be as easy as it sounded in his head.

He had tried to fire the weapon before with his left hand and had not managed the feat. Carter was no gunfighter and never had been. Even when his good hand had been working he had never truly been a sharpshooter.

Soaked in sweat the defiant lawman kept moving through the alleyways. He knew that he had to stop Jonas Stokes from killing even more folks.

Yet Carter had not considered how he was going to answer that daunting challenge. Stokes had one characteristic that the lawman had never possessed.

He was totally insane.

As seconds lengthened into minutes the lawman became no longer afraid of what the next few hours might bring. Carter had resigned himself to the fact that death might in fact be a mercy.

Carter had discovered that none of the people he was paid to protect gave a damn whether he lived or died. He had swallowed his pride and practically begged them for help, but they had remained silent.

Apart from Diamond, Carter was alone. The marshal paused and looked back along the alley. Where was the bounty hunter? he wondered.

Had the shots that he had heard been from Diamond or from the outlaw he chased? Was Johnny Diamond still alive? A chill enveloped Carter.

Doubt began to gnaw at his craw.

If the bounty hunter had fallen victim to the guns of the outlaw that meant that he, Carter, still had three potential killers stalking his every move.

Sweat trailed down from his hatband and ran into his eyes. Carter ran his sleeve across his face as his eyes searched the shadows. Where was the bounty hunter? Diamond had to be dead, he convinced himself.

Suddenly he heard a horse moving beyond the fenced-off yard ahead of him.

Carter froze.

16

Whatever horrific fate Marshal Carter imagined had befallen Johnny Diamond the bounty hunter was far from dead. The tall, thin figure had moved from the narrow alley between the buildings after killing Tom Drury, heading for his tethered horse halfway along the wide street. The moon could not betray him as he walked beneath the porch overhangs towards his weary mount.

The strange lunar illumination cast its eerie light down upon the bodies piled high close to the Long Branch saloon.

As Diamond drew closer to his horse the sight of the dead became clearer. At last, as he came within six feet of his horse, the bounty hunter stopped in his tracks. His eyes focused on the dead.

This was not killing as Diamond

knew of it. This was slaughter. Cold-blooded slaughter on a grand scale.

The bounty hunter vainly tried to reason why anyone would do this. No matter how hard he tried he could not make any sense of it.

He rested his back against the dark wall of the closed saloon and stared in disbelief at the sickening sight, which he had not expected.

His eyes looked up over the pile of corpses at the shattered doorway of the saloon. Diamond ran a thumbnail across his jaw. He wondered if the killer was still inside the saloon, waiting for his next victim.

The bounty hunter had killed more than his fair share of wanted outlaws but he had never murdered innocent folks for the pleasure of it. He blinked hard again and looked down to where the bodies lay.

The moon gave the sight an unreal quality.

Diamond inhaled deeply. The marshal had told him about the man who had arrived in town only minutes earlier on the train from Yuma. The man had held no interest for the bounty hunter until now. Diamond stared hard at the bodies. Each of them had been running. That was easy to tell from the way the corpses were lying on the ground.

A few of them were young males. Some were far older men and two of them were scantily dressed barroom girls. They lay upon one another encircled by a pool of sparkling gore. Frost had already started to gather upon their lifeless forms.

Diamond gritted his teeth.

He had come to Dodge City on the trail of Brewer and Drury and one of them was already dead. His eyes flashed to the opposite end of the street.

Diamond squinted hard. He eased away from the wall but could not see the marshal. The bounty hunter ran a hand over his neck as he slowly moved to the edge of the boardwalk.

He cursed under his breath. Carter

must have gone after Brewer, he thought. The bounty hunter considered the chances of the lawman's surviving an encounter with Sam Brewer.

They were not healthy odds. Brewer was one of the best marksmen in the territory.

Carter was a brave man with a crippled hand.

Diamond was torn as whether he should go after Carter before the lawman bumped into the outlaw or whether he should do as his gut was telling him.

His eyes darted back to the bodies and then the saloon.

In all of his days as a bounty hunter Diamond had always followed the money. He knew it made sense for him to chase the lawman and find Brewer. The outlaw was worth $200.

He stepped towards his horse.

Jonas Stokes was not worth anything as far as the bounty hunter knew. It made no financial sense to go after the mindless killer.

None at all.

Diamond stood next to his horse. He lifted the saddlebags over the cantle and exposed a leather blanket of his own design.

With bony fingers he unbuckled it and peeled back the cover. He pulled away a gleaming, black metal gun from the straps which secured it.

Diamond checked the weapon carefully. As always it was in perfect condition. The long-barrelled gun was fully loaded and ready for action.

He stared at it in his hand. No other six-shooter in the territory had a fourteen-inch barrel, which had been made especially for him by the Colt Company. The bounty hunter had seldom used the weapon but when he had done so the gun had displayed unequalled reliability.

Diamond cocked its hammer and turned to face the saloon.

His eyes narrowed and he started to walk slowly towards the saloon with the unusual weapon held in his hand. Each step brought him closer to the Long Branch.

There was no profit in tackling Stokes.

Johnny Diamond kept walking towards the saloon anyway.

17

Every bone in his body told him he was right. Just beyond the fence that blocked his way Carter could hear the unmistakable sound of a horse being jabbed by its rider's spurs. For some reason the rider was moving up and down one of the back streets. If he was trying to attract the lawman's attention, he was doing a good job. Carter was being lured like a salmon to a fisherman's fly.

Carter moved forward towards the fence.

He pressed his ear up against the unpainted wood and listened. The outlaw was close.

Whoever he was, Carter thought, he was mocking the lawman.

The marshal holstered his gun and stretched to his full height. Carter gripped the very top of the fence with his left hand and hauled himself off the ground. Mustering all his energy he managed to get his right elbow and then his leg over the fence.

He dropped into an unfamiliar yard.

Carter crouched and drew his gun again.

The lawman ran between a stack of empty barrels and reached the back of one of the saloons. He edged his way down a narrow gap between the saloon and another building until he emerged in one of the back streets.

Carter rested between the board-walks.

Suddenly a volley of shots lit up the darkness and the porch beside him was torn apart. Chunks of wood flew in all directions. Carter barely had time to drop to his knees as both buildings were peppered with rifle fire.

More shots rained on the lawman.

The marshal crawled forward and looked under the boardwalk as bullets cut through the darkness. Carter saw the red-hot tapers of lethal lead just before they hit the porch upright above his head.

He was showered in smouldering sawdust. Slivers of burning debris glowed in the darkness like fireflies.

As his clothes smouldered Carter blasted two shots at the horseman in reply. His bullets went wild as the lawman vainly tried to control his gun. Carter edged around the edge of the boardwalk and stared through his gunsmoke at the uninjured rider.

Sam Brewer sat astride his high-shouldered mount with a Winchester in his hands. He was smiling in the moonlight at his vulnerable prey. The lawman knew that the skilled marksman could have killed him at any moment, yet the outlaw was toying with him for some reason.

Carter looked around the back street from his hiding-place for more cover. The street was empty of horses and vehicles. The only cover to be found was where he knelt.

Sam Brewer raised his rifle to his

shoulder and cranked the rifle's mechanism five times in quick succession. Ear-splitting rifle shots tore even more chunks of wood from the porch upright.

Carter coughed as clouds of dust smothered him. He rubbed his face clean with his sleeve and stared at the fearless horseman.

The aroma of burning splinters filled Carter's nostrils as he swung around and blasted his gun a second time at the horseman. Then he frantically crawled back between the buildings to gain more cover.

Carter glanced around the corner and saw the horseman reloading the rifle as he tapped his spurs and slowly advanced towards him.

The lawman felt his throat tighten. He fired the last of his shots at the rider. To his horror none of his bullets had come even close to their target as the tall mount was urged closer.

Unscathed, Brewer was still riding towards him. He was still confident in the marshal's inability to hit him with his bullets. Carter watched as the outlaw cocked the fully loaded rifle again and aimed it in his direction.

Desperately Carter shook the spent shells from his smoking chambers and laid the gun on his lap whilst the fingers of his left hand pulled fresh bullets from his gunbelt and forced them into the weapon.

He tried to reload as quickly as he could but, with only one hand having a full set of fingers, the lawman was hampered.

The sound of the horse's hoofs filled the silent street as he fumbled the last of his bullets into the .45. Awkwardly he completed his labours and turned.

It was too late.

Carter had taken too long to load his weapon.

The moon was at the back of the horseman as he loomed over the kneeling lawman.

Sam Brewer looked down the length of his gleaming barrel at the helpless marshal. The tin star pinned to Carter's chest glinted. For a marksman like Brewer it was a target he could never miss.

'Drop that gun, Marshal,' Brewer ordered.

Marshal Carter stared up at the horseman. He realized that by the time he managed to cock his .45 Brewer could empty the contents of his rifle's magazine into him. The outlaw had the drop on him.

He shook his head. 'Damn it all.'

Brewer glared at his moonlit target. 'You heard me,' he repeated. 'Drop that gun.'

Carter did as he was instructed. Reluctantly he dropped the gun and rose to his feet. He stared at the outlaw and shrugged.

'Now I guess you kill me,' Carter said.

The outlaw threw his head back and laughed out loud. He shook his head.

'Wrong, Marshal. Now I take you to Jonas Stokes.' Brewer paused, then added, 'Then he'll kill you.'

The marshal walked away from the boardwalks and looked into the smoking barrel of the repeating rifle. He stood brooding as his hand pulled the long cigar Diamond had given him. He pushed it between his teeth and then produced a match from his vest.

'Stokes will kill me?' Carter asked. He scratched the match down the bullet-riddled porch upright and touched the end of his cigar.

Brewer nodded. 'He surely will. Jonas has his heart set on it. He holds a grudge and I sure wouldn't care to be in your boots when he starts shooting.'

A cloud of smoke issued from Carter's mouth.

'I ain't feared of dying. Getting yourself killed don't hurt none,' the lawman said. 'Getting wounded hurts far worse.'

Brewer smiled. 'That's what I'm talking about. Jonas intends on making you die real slow, Marshal. He reckons on wounding you over and over again. I figure by the time he's only halfway through to sending you to meet your Maker you'll be begging him to finish you off.'

Carter drew in smoke and pondered.

'Hell!' he cursed. 'That is kinda different.'

18

With no thought for his own safety Johnny Diamond threw himself into the saloon like a puma attacking its prey. He rolled across the bloodstained floor and landed on his boot leather. He held the fourteen-inch-barrelled .45 in his hand and awaited the shots to come from the shadows. But no lethal lead came exploding from the dark interior of the Long Branch in an attempt to add him to its ruthless intruder's already high tally.

Diamond slowly rose up to his full height with his gun held at hip level. The only thing to greet the bounty hunter was an eerie silence. Every instinct he had honed over the years told him that he was alone. There was no sign of Stokes anywhere inside the Long Branch.

All that remained was his monstrous

handiwork. Although it was almost dark in the large bar-room there was enough light filtering through its windows to display every drop of blood that had been spilt. The monster had gone.

Stokes had left the scene of his slayings.

Diamond was angrier than he had ever been. Normally he would not have been drawn into another man's fight, but this seemed different to the bounty hunter.

He wanted to confront Stokes and kill him. Kill him as mercilessly as he had killed all the bodies that now lay around Johnny Diamond.

Even though there was no reward on the head of Jonas Stokes the bounty hunter knew he needed killing.

In the eyes of the law Stokes had no value.

Diamond gazed down at the dead customers surrounding him and knew different. He wandered around the interior of the Long Branch like a bloodhound on a raccoon hunt. He was looking for any sign of life, but all he found were more dead bodies.

Diamond reached over the broken glass which was spread across the bar counter. His fingers sought and found a bottle of whiskey underneath it. He pulled its cork with his teeth, spat it away and lifted the neck of the bottle to his lips.

He swallowed long and hard before resting it down again.

The fiery whiskey burned a trail through his innards as his eyes surveyed the shadows inside the saloon.

The dead were scattered where they had fallen, encircled by pools of dark blood.

Who was this Stokes critter? Diamond wondered, before a more urgent question teased his mind.

Where was Stokes?

Diamond could smell the acrid stench of gun-smoke inside the Long Branch. It was a lingering reminder to the bounty hunter that the most dangerous man he had ever hunted was still alive and still somewhere in Dodge.

Diamond marched back across the body-strewn floorboards towards the gaping doorway. He knew that he had to stop Stokes because there was no one else to do so.

He was about to leave the saloon when his eyes noticed bootprints. They were not his. They led from the saloon, went along the boardwalk and continued towards the end of the long street. Diamond paused at the doorframe and stared at them.

The bounty hunter knelt and ran his fingers across the nearest mark. He straightened up and stared at his fingertips. They were covered in blood.

The bootprints were made by the blood of the bodies inside the Long Branch. Stokes had left the saloon just after he had slain so many of its customers, the bounty hunter told himself. But where had he gone?

Diamond raised his head and wiped his fingers down the front of his well-worn trail coat.

'Where are you?' he muttered.

The dirt of the street was churned up. Wherever the devilish killer had gone was a mystery. The bootprints went to the edge of the boardwalk and then vanished in the ground.

Johnny Diamond stared down the dimly lit thoroughfare. All he could do now was guess. He walked slowly along the boardwalk and then stepped down on to the road.

'Where are you, Stokes?' Diamond whispered, his finger stroking the trigger of his gun.

The words had barely left his lips when a white flash a hundred yards from where he stood lit up the area. The deafening noise of a gun being fired coincided with a pain in his chest.

Diamond was punched by the sudden impact. His thin frame was lifted off his feet and slid across the boardwalk. He crashed into the saloon's front wall and fell to the boards.

No mule could have kicked so

violently or with as much venom as the bullet that had hit his chest. For a moment the bounty hunter just sat against the wall.

He hurt. He hurt badly, but that did not prevent his right hand from raising up and squeezing the trigger of his unique weapon. A plume of white-hot fury exploded through a cloud of smoke as Diamond managed to send his reply. He heard the sound of his bullet hitting the wall close to where the gunman was standing.

The wounded bounty hunter could see the black shadow of the gunman running up the rise towards the railhead. Stokes ran halfway up the slope, then he turned and fired again. Diamond sat against the wall and watched as the bullet fell short and kicked up dust ten feet ahead of him.

The bounty hunter gritted his teeth and raised his gun once more.

He blasted his gun and watched as the assassin was forced to duck as Diamond's own bullet went over his head. The wounded man had more than enough range with his customized weapon. Satisfied, Diamond grunted.

Diamond pressed his hand against the wound. He arched in agony. Then he forced his reluctant eyes to stare down at the boardwalk beneath him.

There was more blood now.

Diamond watched as the bloody bootprints were swamped by the new stream of gore. Blood trailed down from his chest on to his leg and dripped through the gaps in the boards.

The wounded bounty hunter rolled on to his side. Somehow he managed to raise himself up on to his knees and then he forced his shaking legs to stand. He stared down at the blood that covered the boardwalk.

It was his blood.

It was the blood of Johnny Diamond.

19

Sam Brewer hauled his reins back. The startling sound of the shots resonated in Brewer's and Carter's ears. The outlaw's face went blank as the reports echoed around him and his prisoner. Sam Brewer held his reins in check and looked ahead towards the corner of Front Street. He began to wonder where Drury was and what Jonas Stokes was up to. Stokes had hired him and Drury to help him avenge himself on the lawman, yet he seemed to be willing to slaughter anyone who got in his way. The horseman did not like plans that changed without warning.

Ben Carter turned round and looked up at his mounted oppressor. It was the first time the lawman had seen a chink in the outlaw's armour. Brewer actually looked concerned. A shadow of doubt now filled the outlaw's mind.

'What's wrong, son?' Carter asked wistfully. 'You look mighty troubled. How come?'

Brewer had no answers; only a tidal wave of questions that grew with every moment he was forced to spend in this shambles of a town. Anxiously he bit his lip.

Brewer was feeling utterly bewildered. He was used to striking quickly and then high-tailing it. This was taking far too long for his liking. The outlaw knew that the longer his kind hung around in places like Dodge the more danger they were in.

The unarmed Carter kept on walking towards the corner. The rider spurred and caught up with his captive. The lawman looked over his shoulder.

'There's nothing to be troubled about,' Carter said.

Brewer slid his rifle into its saddle scabbard and drew one of his guns. His eyes darted frantically from one menacing shadow to the next.

'Hush up, Marshal,' he drawled.

The lawman turned and smiled at Brewer. 'It's only someone shooting, boy.'

Brewer searched vainly for a cigar. 'I told you to hush up, Marshal. Savvy?'

Sensing nervousness in the rider Carter turned the corner. The outlaw, standing in his stirrups, rode just behind him. The two men continued down the long street. Every fifty feet or so one of the street lanterns glowed and yet it remained in a twilight world, somewhere between darkness and light. Circles of amber light were dotted down the long street beneath each of the high poles.

'You're thinking that Stokes fired them shots,' Carter said over his shoulder. 'But did he? Are you sure enough to bet your hide on that, son?'

Brewer lowered himself on to his saddle. 'Sure it was Stokes, old-timer. Who else would it be?'

Carter kept on walking. 'It could have been anyone. There are a lot of guns in Dodge. All it takes is for one critter to find the courage to face

Stokes and start fanning his gun hammer. For all you know he's dead.'

Brewer was thoughtful. 'Shut up, old-timer. I ain't in the mood to start playing games.'

The lawman stopped and turned to face the rider of the high-shouldered horse. Carter rested his knuckles on his gunbelt and looked at the troubled outlaw.

'What if it ain't Stokes doing all the shooting we heard?' Carter suggested.

Brewer pointed his gun at the lawman.

'I told you to hush the hell up,' he snarled.

'It might even be the bounty hunter,' Carter suggested.

Brewer held his horse on a tight rein. His eyes glared down at the smiling face of the lawman.

'What do you know about a bounty hunter, Marshal?' he asked, training his six-shooter on the lawman.

'I know he's in town to kill you and your partner,' Carter stated.

Brewer thought about Swifty Davis,

the man he and Drury had paid to kill the bounty hunter who had been trailing them for two long days and nights. Had the bounty hunter managed to evade him?

'We left a man out there in the desert to bushwhack the varmint,' Brewer growled as his icy glare burned down on the marshal. 'Nobody could have gotten past him. Nobody.'

Carter lowered his head. 'He did.'

Brewer looked even more troubled. 'He did?'

The lawman gave a slow nod. 'He sure did.'

The outlaw looked all around him and gripped his reins tightly in his free hand.

'Where's the bastard now?'

'He's in town,' Carter told him. He sucked on his cigar and blew smoke at the rider. 'He's gunning for you and your partner. Where is your partner, anyway? Where is he?'

Brewer looked around the buildings on both sides of the streets. There was no sign of Drury. He edged his mount closer to the marshal.

'What do you know about Tom?' he snarled.

'I know that Johnny Diamond has his heart set on claiming the reward money on both your heads,' Carter replied. 'I reckon that he might just do it. He seemed quite a capable fella.'

The outlaw mulled over the name that the lawman had just uttered. It was a name he had heard before and one which sent a chill into his soul.

'Johnny Diamond?' Brewer gasped. 'Is that the varmint who's been tailing us?'

Carter nodded.

'And he's gunning for you and your pal.' The lawman gripped the cigar firmly in his teeth. 'By my reckoning he's already earned himself two hundred dollars by killing one of you. It's only a matter of time before he wants the other two hundred and comes after you.'

Brewer lowered his eyebrows. He frowned.

'Where is Diamond?'

'That I don't know,' Carter admitted.

'Try and think, old man,' Brewer threatened. 'I'll surely shoot you if you don't.'

The lawman knew he was sailing close to the wind. Brewer was troubled and men are dangerous when they get troubled, he thought.

'The last time I saw him he was heading over yonder after your pal.' Carter pointed to the other side of the street. 'There was a lot of gunplay and I ain't seen him since.'

Suddenly Brewer realized that the lawman was probably speaking the truth. Drury had ridden in that direction. He rubbed his face and glanced over the lawman to the distant saloon. Even from the opposite end of Front Street Brewer could see the dead bodies.

'Start walking again,' the outlaw ordered.

Carter nodded and pulled his cigar from his lips.

'We headed anywhere in particular, boy?' he asked.

The twisted face of Sam Brewer was like that of a snarling wolf. He spat anger at his defenceless prisoner.

'Just walk, old-timer,' Brewer snarled. 'You'll find out where we're headed soon enough unless I kill you first.'

Ben Carter removed the cigar from his lips and dropped it on the ground. He crushed it with his boot heel, then began to obey his instructions.

Brewer kept tapping his bloody spurs against the flank of his mount. He remained only a few feet behind the lawman as they continued along Front Street in the direction of the railroad terminal.

With each step that he took Carter felt as if he were heading towards his own executioner. He glanced up at the church clock.

It was only twenty-five minutes after eight.

It seemed far later.

20

Jonas Stokes was down to his last few bullets after leaving a pile of bodies in his murderous wake. The ruthless killer had been making his way back to the railroad ticket office to get more ammunition from his canvas bag when he spotted the tall bounty hunter. Stokes had been unable to resist adding one more notch on his six-shooter's grip and opened up on Johnny Diamond. After seeing the bounty hunter knocked off his feet and crashing into the front wall of the saloon the determined killer blasted one more shot at the fallen Diamond.

When his bullet fell short of its target Stokes reasoned that he was out of range. Then, to his utter surprise, the bounty hunter had levelled his own unique six-shooter at him and fired a shot, which had flown past his head.

Stokes vowed to return and finish off the bounty hunter when he had replenished his guns and belt with fresh ammunition.

The last thing Diamond had seen of his opponent was the man running up to the train depot. The bounty hunter was pumping blood from his chest wound as he staggered along the boardwalk and was about to enter the Long Branch. Diamond paused at the doorframe and rested his bloody left hand upon the splintered wood.

The bounty hunter watched as droplets of his blood fell on to the boardwalk with every beat of his pounding heart. His mind raced as he held his smoking gun against his leg.

Mustering every last ounce of his strength he glanced into the interior of the saloon. His eyes focused on the whiskey bottle on top of the counter and he forced himself towards it.

Racked by pain Diamond staggered between the bodies inside the saloon towards his goal. He pushed the long barrel of his gun into his belt as he reached his objective.

The burning he felt in his back told Diamond that the vicious bullet had ripped right through him. He grabbed the bottle of rye off the bar counter and poured it over his chest and then down his neck and over his back.

The bounty hunter arched in agony as the fiery contents of the bottle burned into his torn flesh. For a few moments Diamond just stood still as he felt the hard liquor cleanse his horrific injury.

He gritted his teeth and was ready to drop when the sound of spurs made Diamond raise his head.

This was not over, his mind screamed at him.

Diamond ignored his injuries, snatched his Colt from his belt and ran across the saloon to where the door lay on the sawdust-covered floor.

The bounty hunter gritted his teeth and narrowed his eyes.

The first thing to catch his blurred

eyes was the tin star on Carter's vest. It gleamed in the moonlight. Diamond pulled the hammer of his gun back until the sound of it fully locking filled his ears.

He shook his head and tried to clear his eyes.

The sight of the rider just behind the lawman confused the wounded bounty hunter for a moment. Diamond rubbed his eyes again and then saw the gun in the horseman's hand.

It was aimed straight at Carter.

Diamond pushed his injured body away from the doorframe and moved to the wooden porch upright. He screwed up his eyes and stared across the hundred yards to the approaching pair.

After what felt like a lifetime to Diamond the horseman's face came into focus. The bounty hunter lifted his gun arm and levelled the long-barrelled Colt at Sam Brewer.

The weary bounty hunter stared down the gun's sights at the outlaw and squeezed back on his trigger.

A deafening report and a flash spewed from the end of the fourteen-inch barrel and lit up the street. Carter instinctively ducked as the red-hot taper burst from the cloud of smoke that encircled the barrel.

Sam Brewer watched in stunned awe as the shot flew past him. Without even thinking the outlaw steadied his spooked mount and fired back.

Johnny Diamond swung his lean frame around as the outlaw's bullet embedded itself in the upright. A black chunk of wood was torn away as the bounty hunter cocked and fired his .45 again at the outlaw.

The bullet cut through the cool night air and narrowly missed its target.

Brewer felt the heat of the bullet scorch past him. He leapt from his saddle and threw himself at the lawman. The outlaw wrestled Carter around the neck and swung him around to face the bounty hunter.

Diamond frowned as he cocked his

gun hammer again. His usually keen-witted mind was swimming inside his skull.

His target was now hiding behind the lawman. Brewer was using Carter as a human shield. The outlaw fired his gun again as his other arm held Carter around the shoulder and neck.

The bounty hunter moved again.

The porch upright was riddled with lead and yet Diamond fearlessly refused to find better cover. He stood his ground and glanced through the cloud of dense smoke as Brewer fired yet more shots at him.

The bounty hunter did not flinch as his Stetson was ripped from his head and rolled down the bloody boardwalk. Instead he dragged one of his other holstered guns from his belt and tossed it to Carter.

'Here you are, Marshal,' Diamond shouted loudly. 'Here's a gun for you.'

The six-shooter landed at the feet of the outlaw and the lawman.

'Damn it all, Marshal,' Diamond

cursed. 'I meant for you to catch that gun.'

As the outlaw held the marshal in check he saw the gleaming handgun land at their feet. He raised his own Colt and squeezed on its trigger. The hammer fell on a spent bullet. The hollow noise filled his ears. No matter how many times he pulled on his trigger there were no longer any fresh bullets in his smoking weapon.

Brewer was totally confused.

He stared at the empty gun in his hand in horror. How could he reload his six-shooter with only one hand? His attention returned to the .45 at their feet.

The outlaw had a choice to make.

He made it.

Diamond watched as the outlaw released his grip on Carter and dropped to the ground. Brewer eagerly scooped the .45 off the ground. The lawman watched helplessly as Diamond eased away from the porch upright and stepped down from the boardwalk.

Ben Carter was stunned by the bounty hunter's apparently suicidal act. He waved his hands frantically, trying to stop the wounded man from striding through the moonlight.

'No, Diamond. Don't.'

Diamond did not look at the lawman. He glared furiously at the kneeling outlaw before him.

On his knees Sam Brewer cocked the gun hammer of the fresh weapon and aimed it at the tall figure who was marching towards him.

'You're gonna die. Say goodbye to life, Diamond.' Brewer laughed as he squeezed on the trigger. The laughter faded as a sudden realization dawned upon the outlaw. The clicking noise of an empty gun again filled his ears. His eyes focused on the gun. 'What the hell?'

Brewer's stunned expression made the bounty hunter smile as he paced towards the wanted outlaw. Diamond cocked his own hammer and raised his gun. He aimed the .45 at Brewer and fired.

Coldly Diamond stared at Brewer as blood streamed down from the bullet hole in his shirt. There was no life in the outlaw's pained expression.

A gut-wrenching groan came from him.

The outlaw rocked on his knees and then fell face first upon the ground. Blood spread away from the dead body and surrounded it like a satanic halo.

Diamond turned and walked to where the stunned Carter stood. He reached the lawman's side and began to reload the lethal weapon in his hand.

'Are you OK?' Diamond asked Carter.

'I'm fine, but you don't look so good.' Carter reached down and pulled the gun from Brewer's dead hand. He started to load it from the bullets on his own belt. 'Are you OK, Diamond?'

Johnny Diamond turned and stared back at the rail depot.

'I will be,' he whispered.

The town marshal gripped hold of

the bounty hunter's arm and drew his full attention.

'This is my fight,' Carter insisted. 'Not yours. You've done your work. This is my problem. Stokes only came to Dodge to kill me.'

Diamond pointed at his bloodstained shirt.

'This made it personal, Marshal. You want to tag along, then start walking. I intend killing that bastard.'

21

The stationmaster stared at the gruesome face through his small office window. Stokes leaned forward and waved one of his guns at the elderly man. Slowly the old man's hands rose upward as the grim reality of his situation dawned upon him.

'Who are you?' the stationmaster asked. 'What do you want of me?'

Stokes reached through the narrow gap and grabbed the collar of the terrified railroad man.

'My bag,' he growled. 'Get me my damn bag.'

The canvas bag had no sooner been handed to the cruel Stokes than the stationmaster felt a sudden jolt, which pushed him backwards. As he closed the window and turned towards the lamplight he noticed the knife protruding from his belly. He staggered forwards and crashed into the table and chairs.

Stokes had what he wanted. He unfastened the grip on the bag and hauled out his box of bullets. His skilled hands made short work of replenishing his gunbelt and weapons.

The railroad depot was quiet as Stokes walked from the buildings and started back down into the heart of bloodstained Dodge City. He held both his guns in his hands and moved through the shadows back down the slope. He was ready to finish the job that he had started. Stokes was ready to kill Carter and anyone else who got in his way.

Stokes looked down into the gloom.

Dodge was different from when he had arrived only thirty minutes before. Now every store was shuttered. Every light that had spilled out on to Front Street had been extinguished. Apart from the dim street lanterns only the eerie light from the moon illuminated the town.

Stokes marched down through the shadows boldly and without any doubt in his rancid mind that what he was going to do was just. Revenge was a powerful emotion, which he was unable and also unwilling to ignore. He had filled both his guns with the bullets from the ammunition box and then cast his canvas bag aside.

Killing had become even easier to Stokes than it had been before he was imprisoned. Now it was so easy that like a rabid dog his lust for destruction grew with every passing moment.

Stokes moved through the blackness of night and stopped beside the livery stables.

He had just reached the large, wide-open doors when he saw the two men heading towards it. For a moment Stokes thought that they were Brewer and Drury. Then, as his eyes narrowed, he saw the truth. The gleaming tin star pinned to Carter's chest glittered in the moonlight and betrayed its wearer. The taller man had to be a deputy, Stokes presumed. The loathsome killer cocked the hammers of both his .45s and fired.

Two bullets sped through the shadows at both Carter and Diamond. Both men ducked as the shots passed over their heads.

Carter dragged his companion off the street and pushed the bounty hunter up against the side wall of a saloon as another two shots lit up the darkness.

Diamond gritted his teeth and looked at the lawman as he struggled with the gun in his hand.

'Calm down, Marshal,' Diamond said. 'Your hand will do what it has to do. Just give it a chance.'

Carter nodded at the bounty hunter, raised his left hand and fired. The bullet hit the large, open stable door.

'Lucky shot, Marshal.' Diamond winked as he drew his long-range weapon and pulled back on its hammer. He raised his arm over the lawman's head and squeezed its trigger.

Stokes was behind the stable door as

the bounty hunter's bullet ripped right through its wooden panels. The killer looked at the big bullet hole, only a few inches above his head, and backed into the livery.

'He's gone in the stable. Now's our chance,' Diamond snarled as he raced along the boardwalk with the marshal at his heels. Both men ducked into the recess of the hardware store as another shot came blasting at them. Stokes was firing from between the hinges and the doorframe.

No sooner had a chunk of the window frame been ripped from the storefront than the bounty hunter swung back out on to the boardwalk and fired his long-barrelled weapon again. His bullet punched another hole in the large wooden door.

'C'mon, Marshal,' the bounty hunter yelled out as he ran towards the livery stable with his gun in his outstretched hand. He fired again and then dropped to his knees beside a trough. Carter flung himself against the wall of a tailor's shop and squeezed his own trigger. The big livery-stable doors shook as more holes were punched into them.

Jonas Stokes moved deeper into the large livery.

His eyes darted around its huge interior. A glowing forge in the corner cast a scarlet light throughout the cavernous building. Stokes spun on his heels as two more shots rocked the big door again. Moonlight streamed in through the holes in the door as Stokes moved to where a number of skittish horses stood in their stalls.

He raised both guns and fired again at the door.

Stokes knew that he was being hemmed in. He looked around the livery for a side door. There was none.

The devious mind of the wanton killer raced. He crouched beside the stalls as two further shots came from the guns of the sheriff and his companion.

Shafts of moonlight moved across the

floor of the livery as the door swung inward.

Stokes looked around and saw the wooden ladder. He straightened up and stared up into the hayloft. A devilish smile played over his features. Without even thinking Stokes rammed one of his smoking guns into its holster and raced to the ladder.

He started to climb. He would fire down on to his enemies, he thought. Like a matador he would sink his swords into the necks of the raging bulls.

Stokes had barely reached the top of the ladder when Carter and Diamond came bursting in to the livery. Both men stopped when they saw the figure of their adversary clambering over the edge of the loft.

Carter held the gun in his shaking hand and was about to fire when Stokes managed to twist on the last rung of the ladder and shoot down at them. The gun was torn from Carter's hand. The lawman stared at his hand and gasped in relief as he saw that he still had all his fingers.

Then suddenly Diamond groaned and buckled beside him. The concerned lawman reached out to his cohort and held the bounty hunter before he collapsed.

'What's wrong, Diamond?' Carter asked anxiously.

Diamond shook his head and raised a hand to his still-bleeding bullet wound.

'It's this damn bullet hole in my chest.' Diamond winced as pain tore through him. 'I'm finished, Marshal. I can't keep going.'

Carter glanced up at Stokes and then back at Diamond. The bounty hunter dropped to his knees and forced the long-barrelled weapon into the lawman's hand.

'Take this and finish that critter,' Diamond urged. 'You can do it. You just gotta have faith in yourself.'

Before the marshal could say anything he heard a shot and felt the shirt ripped from his shoulder. Ben Carter turned and raised the big gun in his left hand.

He pulled the trigger.

The kick of the gun knocked him backwards and he landed on the seat of his pants next to the bounty hunter. Carter cocked the gun again and was about to fire when he saw the stunned expression on Stokes's face high above them on the edge of the hayloft.

Stokes swayed as life ebbed from him.

The light from the glowing forge danced across his face as the gun fell from his hand. A few seconds after the weapon hit the dirt the doomed killer followed it.

Both the marshal and the bounty hunter watched silently as Stokes tumbled head-first from the high loft.

Every horse in the livery stable bucked and shied when the body crashed into the ungiving ground. Stokes tried to rise, then he gave out a hideous gasp as what was left of his existence evaporated from his broken body.

Both his onlookers watched as the deadly bandit lay in the middle of the livery.

'He's dead, Diamond.' Carter swallowed hard in amazed excitement. 'I killed the critter.'

Johnny Diamond accepted the return of his prized weapon and smiled at the lawman.

'Mighty fancy shooting for a one-handed star-packer,' Diamond remarked. 'You done good, old-timer.'

'I reckon I got lucky,' Carter replied and sighed thankfully.

The bounty hunter nodded.

'Now, if you're through patting yourself on the back, I'd be mighty obliged if you'd go get me a sawbones, Marshal,' Diamond said weakly. He pressed his hand against the bullet wound. 'I surely need tending real bad.'

Finale

The morning sun cast its brilliant light down upon the bloodstained streets of Dodge City. It was a new day in more ways than one. The streets were busy again as if nothing had happened but as the townsfolk went about their daily rituals not one of them looked or spoke to the battle-weary Carter.

The entire town had expected him to die when Stokes arrived in Dodge. They could not conceal their disappointment at the outcome.

Ben Carter walked from his office boardwalk and made his way down the street towards the stagecoach depot. He looked at the church clock for a moment, then proceeded towards his goal.

Before the lawman reached the stagecoach depot he paused outside the small office of Doc Hardy and looked at the medical man's shingle. He considered walking up to the door to find out how the bounty hunter was doing after their ordeal but then he doubted the wisdom of such curiosity. What would be gained by doing that? Carter thought.

Slowly Carter continued on towards the stagecoach depot. Throughout the night he had pondered on many things until by dawn he had made his decision.

He had barely taken three steps when he heard the familiar voice of Johnny Diamond call out to him.

Carter stopped and turned.

To his amazement the bounty hunter was walking from the doctor's office. Carter smiled at the taller and younger man as he approached.

'Hell, Diamond. I thought you were a goner when I dragged your sorrowful carcass in there last night,' the marshal said with a grin as he patted Diamond's shoulder.

Diamond smiled. He pulled two

cigars from his pocket and rammed one into his own mouth, the other into Carter's.

'The bullet went clean through,' Diamond explained as he struck a match and lit both of their smokes. 'The doc sewed me up and gave me a clean bill of health.'

'That's mighty fine,' Carter said through a cloud of cigar smoke. 'I'm pleased for you.'

Diamond studied Carter as he too inhaled on his cigar.

'I'm grateful for the reward money you left with the doc, Marshal,' he said. 'I was down to my last three dollars.'

'You earned that bounty and a lot more,' Carter told him. He walked on, now with his new friend beside him.

'Where you going, Marshal?' Diamond asked.

Carter turned to face the bounty hunter.

'I reckon you best start calling me Carter,' he advised.

'I don't understand.' Diamond rubbed

his chin. 'What do you mean?'

'I ain't a marshal any more, Diamond.' Carter pointed to his vest. The tin star was no longer pinned to it. 'I quit after I sorted out your bounty money.'

The bounty hunter tilted his head. 'Why?'

Carter looked at the many faces in the street. None of them looked in his direction.

'I figured something out last night,' Carter said. 'I asked folks to help me when I learned that Stokes was headed to Dodge to kill me. Not one of the menfolk in this whole town even bothered to help.'

'Why not?' Diamond wondered.

'Who knows?' Carter shrugged and blew smoke at the air. 'Maybe they just don't like me.'

Diamond laughed.

Carter and Diamond continued on their way. They reached the stagecoach depot where Carter stopped. The bounty hunter was thoughtful.

'Did any of these critters in town ever notice you had a crippled hand?' he questioned.

'I kept it pretty well hid.'

'Not from me.' Diamond raised an eyebrow. 'I spotted it straight away.'

'You surely did.' Carter smiled.

The stagecoach came rolling into the street. It pulled up against the depot boardwalk. Two passengers disembarked, then Ben Carter stepped into the coach and sat down. The bounty hunter slammed the carriage door shut.

'Where are you going, Carter?' Diamond asked through the window.

Carter pulled out a long strip of tickets he had purchased earlier that morning and stared at them.

'I'm taking the stagecoach to Waco Wells.' He grinned.

'What the hell for?'

'Damned if I know, friend.' Carter smiled and then gripped the cigar between his teeth. 'I've got an inkling that it ought to be a whole lot quieter than it is here, though.'

Both men touched the brims of their hats in salute to one another as the depot manager handed the mailbag up to the guard.

The driver released his brake pole, cracked his reins down across the backs of his team and steered the stagecoach away from the boardwalk.

Johnny Diamond watched as the stagecoach started down the long, bloodstained street.

He scratched his chin and smiled.

'Where'd I leave my damn horse?' he asked himself. Then he spotted the neglected animal across the street at a hitching rail. He marched towards it. Diamond pulled the long leathers free, mounted the animal and reasoned: 'I reckon I might take me a ride to Waco Wells as well. Least I'll have me one friend there.'

Johnny Diamond spurred in pursuit of the stagecoach.

FORTRESS PALOMINO
TO KILL THE VALKO KID
KID FURY

We do hope that you have enjoyed reading this large print book.

Did you know that all of our titles are available for purchase?

We publish a wide range of high quality large print books including:
Romances, Mysteries, Classics
General Fiction
Non Fiction and Westerns

Special interest titles available in large print are:
The Little Oxford Dictionary
Music Book, Song Book
Hymn Book, Service Book

Also available from us courtesy of Oxford University Press:
Young Readers' Dictionary
(large print edition)
Young Readers' Thesaurus
(large print edition)

For further information or a free brochure, please contact us at:
Ulverscroft Large Print Books Ltd.,
The Green, Bradgate Road, Anstey,
Leicester, LE7 7FU, England.
Tel: (00 44) **0116 236 4325**
Fax: (00 44) **0116 234 0205**

Other titles in the
Linford Western Library:

BADMAN SHERIFF

Simon Webb

When the citizens of Coopers Creek elect Ned Turner as their sheriff, they are blind to the deadly mistake being made. For Turner is a lawless rogue seeking to exploit the position for his own advantage. It will be left to mild-mannered baker Jack Crawley to set things right. But can he rescue his town from the worst badman sheriff Montana has ever known?

LEGEND OF THE DEAD MEN'S GOLD

I. J. Parnham

Ten years ago, the Helliton gang holed up in a stronghold with a stolen wagonload of gold. One year later, all of them were dead — fallen defending their hoard from other outlaws, and fighting amongst themselves. The last living gang member cursed the gold, saying that if he couldn't have it, nobody would. Or so the legend goes . . . Trip Kincaid had always been fascinated by the tale. His brother Oliver suspects it's the true reason behind his sudden disappearance — and is determined to find him . . .